MANCHESTER UNCANNY

FROM THE REVIEWS OF *LONDON GOTHIC*

'Flatly deadpan implications blossoming... haunting... continuously relishable... Hitchcockian... seminal... provocative...' D.F. Lewis, *Gestalt Real-Time Reviews*

'Royle is a master of the uncanny. His stories abound with half-glimpsed horrors, strange doubles, phantom sounds and messages from the dead' Joe Darlington, *Manchester Review of Books*

'Cumulatively, the stories in *London Gothic* map out our contemporary anxieties, our fragile sense of who we are as individuals and as a society, that sense of disruption and fragmentation made explicit by Brexit and Covid. These are stories that speak to, even "infect" each other, like virulent examples of *mise en abîme*... Loneliness, insanity, lovelessness, purposelessness, obliteration, are all just around the corner, and the truth is that we can't bear to think about them. And yet, as Royle – a unique stylist and teller of genuinely unsettling stories – demonstrates, we do' Mike O'Driscoll, *Ginger Nuts of Horror*

'A pervasive sense of dread...' Sarah Johnson, *Horrified*

'Subtly probes the urban cracks' Lydia Bunt, *Review 31*

'This collection evidences that Royle is not only a vital advocate of the short story, but is himself a master of the form' Melissa Wan, *Medium*

'Alongside an undercurrent of the macabre there is much humour... Fabulous, at times chilling, storytelling to curl up with as the evenings draw in' Jackie Law, *neverimitate*

'One of the best short story collections I've read in years' Stephen Bacon

'Mastery of voice and point of view. If you like stories that combine cleverness with direction, this collection reads as a masterclass of the form' Richard Clegg, *Manchester Review*

MANCHESTER UNCANNY

SHORT STORIES

NICHOLAS ROYLE

First published in the UK in 2022 by Cōnfingō Publishing

249 Burton Road, Didsbury, Manchester M20 2WA

www.confingopublishing.uk

Cover design by Zoë McLean

Typesetting by John Oakey

Printed by TJ Books Limited

A CIP catalogue record for this book is available from the British Library

ISBN 978-1-7399614-7-3

2 4 6 8 10 9 7 5 3 1

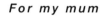

For my mum

CONTENTS

Welcome Back

The signs had been there from the start.

I was on Richard's presentation panel. If you apply for a job at the university and you get shortlisted, you have to submit to two panels: an interview panel and a presentation panel. The interview panel might be chaired by Maeve, the head of department, and the presentation panel by someone lesser, like me, for example. The findings of the presentation panel have to be communicated, after all the presentations have taken place, to the interview panel, who, in my experience, take no notice of the presentation panel's findings and hire whoever they have already decided to hire, for whatever reasons, sometimes even the right ones.

It wasn't like this in my day.

My interview amounted to a brief chat with three people, the then head of department, the then academic director and the then dean. I heard myself talking about short stories and the dean asked who I liked and I went blank. I couldn't think of anyone I liked who I thought she would also like, or at least have heard of. Let's change the question, she said. Who is the best short story writer in the world? Again, blank. If it helps, she went on, there is a right answer.

It didn't.

The answer, she said, is Alice Munro.

As it happened, I had just read Alice Munro's latest collection. I think I was reviewing it. I had admired it without enjoying it. Often you say you've enjoyed something, don't you? Thank you for sending me your story. I enjoyed reading it, but it's not a good fit for the magazine. Thank you for sending me your novel. I enjoyed reading it, but it's not quite right for the list. It's a way to avoid saying you didn't think it was very good. In the case of Alice Munro, however, while I can agree that she's good, I don't enjoy reading her. The stories are often too long for my taste. They're more like condensed novels than short stories. The interrelationships between the characters are overly complex and require too much explanation. I said something like this to the dean and for some reason they still offered me the job.

Richard was the last shortlisted candidate we saw. He came in and sat down and launched into some anecdote, possibly prompted, possibly not – I can't remember. I can't remember what he said or why he said it, but I remember very clearly what happened next. He looked at us, his lifeless gaze alighting on each of us in turn, and said, But you wouldn't understand. I do remember that we looked at each other. If the others were thinking what I was thinking, then we were wondering what we had in common for Richard to make such a presumption about us. We all had jobs and we all had air in our lungs and blood in our veins.

I checked with my colleagues, wrote up my notes and took the panel's findings to the interview panel. We were not recommending that Richard be hired – indeed, he had come bottom out of the half-dozen candidates who had presented to us – and not because of the casual way in which he had prejudged us, but because his presentation had not been very good.

He was, of course, offered the job.

I very much hope I won't have to work with him, I said, crossly, rashly and perhaps somewhat self-righteously, to Maeve, having already given her the necessary context. Of course not, she said.

So when it happened, the thing that happened later, perhaps it shouldn't have been surprising, but it still took me by surprise.

This was months, even years later. Time had acquired the quality of liquid soap. The pandemic had started – and gone on. There had been one lockdown, maybe two. Predictably, despite the assurance Maeve had given me, Richard was working under me, as one of a number of colleagues delivering workshop. I was the leader of the module. We had had some perfectly normal interactions: he had asked me for advice on how to do this or that, which I had given him. In addition, I had been asked to review his novel, anonymously, for the pre-REF exercise. I had given it three stars, knowing they would increase it to four, which they did. Then, in workshop, he advised one of his students, who was writing experimental short stories, that he should do something else. No one publishes that kind of thing, he said to the student. And, anyway, it's not really working. This was all online; everything was online at that point.

Richard emailed me to let me know that this had happened and that the student was unhappy. The student and I exchanged emails. Richard and I exchanged emails. I politely pointed out to Richard that it was our role to encourage and support the students in whatever they wanted to write. We weren't one of those places that made them write in a particular style or genre. I wasn't even sure they even existed, those places, but they certainly existed in the popular, or, perhaps more accurately, the critical imagination, which held that creative writing students were being churned out of universities like sausages out of factories, all writing the same kind of thing in the same way. We assessed applicants on the quality of their writing and offered places mostly on the strength of that, so it would be unhelpful if, once they started, we discouraged them from writing the kind of thing they wanted to write. I wondered who had given this student his place. I looked him up; it had been me. Maybe I was more of a fan of experimental short stories than Richard was, but that also meant I knew that there were publishers who did publish this kind of stuff and I emailed Richard to tell him this, again politely, respectfully, like I email everyone. I treat everyone the same. That's what I was brought up to do and it just kind of stuck.

Richard's response moved things on a little. He didn't feel he was the best tutor for this student. So I asked the student if he wanted to move to a different group. I could organise that easily and quickly, I told him. No, thank you, he wrote back. He liked the group and didn't want to move.

He was still unhappy, however, with the advice that had been given and the way in which it had been delivered and, as everyone working in the sector was now well aware, students' wishes and feelings, ever since the introduction of tuition fees had effectively transformed lecturers from educators into service providers, had become of paramount importance. At certain times of the year, Maeve's entire working day seemed to consist of sending out emails to colleagues urging us to encourage our students to fill in and return the latest student survey.

Right. I think we've reached an impasse, I wrote to my husband in a text. Looks like it, he texted back. What are you going to do?

I felt that having reached this point there was only one thing I could do. I wrote to Richard and explained that the student liked the group and didn't want to move, so I had been trying to think of a way to make that possible and for everyone to be happy, which was all I wanted, after all. I asked Richard how he would feel about apologising to the student.

It didn't seem like a big deal to me, but rather the simplest way to resolve the situation and allow things to carry on as they had before.

So, as I say, I wasn't expecting Richard's response.

You seem to have believed the student, Richard wrote. That is not surprising.

I wanted to stop and think about that line, but could see there was more to come and I had a bad feeling about it, so I read on.

I didn't hear anything about Richard for three months after that. It was like he was a ghost. I asked a few people, a few times, but they either feigned ignorance or genuinely didn't know what was going on.

There had been a flurry of email activity following Richard's last message to me. I had copied all the relevant correspondence to Maeve and to Ravi, the course leader. Both had reassured me that I hadn't done anything wrong. It hadn't occurred to me that I might have done, but nevertheless, in the circumstances, it was reassuring. It's always good to know that people have your back. No one wants to drive – or to appear to have driven – a colleague to quit their job. But nor does anyone want to receive an email like the one Richard sent me, which basically said how dare I suggest he apologise to a student and I should never write to him again and he would be handing in his resignation the following day.

It wasn't until my performance review with Maeve three months later that I found out what had – or hadn't – happened after that.

She made no mention of Richard during the performance review until we had more or less finished and I said I had a question. I didn't know whether Richard had quit and had departed or was perhaps working out his notice, or whether he had changed his mind, or what. Maeve took a deep breath, then embarked on a curious and long-winded speech. I very soon lost the thread. It had the feeling of a speech she had rehearsed but had never quite got off pat, relying on her experience and on her confidence that she could come across as a worker rather than a manager, that she could employ her natural charm to avoid sounding like a government minister insisting that we're all in it together. I was able to pick a few bones out of it: Richard had tendered his resignation, but the university had bent over backwards to try to persuade him to stay. That process of negotiation, it seemed, was still ongoing. I had to understand that Richard had had a difficult time and had experienced a lot of injustice and prejudice. I said I understood that, but I was left with a strong sense that 'You haven't done anything wrong' had been kind of watered down to something like 'You haven't *really* done anything wrong'.

If it had been another one of my colleagues who had got into this situation, I said to Maeve, I would have said the same thing, in the same way.

I understand that, said Maeve, but they won't necessarily have had the same set of experiences.

I never assume that anyone has had the same set of experiences as the next person, I said. I speak to everyone the same way.

But I think we need to recognise, Maeve said, that formerly living colleagues are likely to have had a very particular set of experiences.

So, are you saying, I asked, dropping a mental pin on

Maeve's use of a term that some now regarded as offensive, that we need to speak to dead colleagues differently?

I had been looking off to the side for most of the conversation, once I had brought the subject around to Richard, but now I was looking at Maeve's face on the screen. I wondered if she had frozen, or gone on mute, but she was just taking a moment. Trying to work out how to respond, I imagined. Her mouth was open and her face was apparently in the middle of adopting the expression of someone doing their best to express nuance.

I just think it's time to recognise, she said, that formerly living colleagues may have faced a particular set of experiences.

I spent the summer saving historical emails from Maeve and Ravi – and from Richard – while at the same time deleting hundreds of other old emails in order to comply with the university's barrage of emails telling me, Your mailbox is almost full. Please reduce your mailbox size.

If they didn't keep sending me those emails, I said to my husband, perhaps my mailbox would not be almost full.

I had heard a rumour that Richard had finally left his teaching job, but that the university had succeeded in not quite letting go of him, by making him a visiting professor or an honorary fellow or whatever the exact term was for someone who would probably not be paid anything but would continue to be associated with the institution, an arrangement likely to be mutually convenient and beneficial. Perhaps this shouldn't have bothered me and perhaps it wouldn't have done if I had heard about it from either Maeve or Ravi rather than on the grapevine. Although perhaps it would have done, since it still bothered me that Richard had as good as accused me of deathism with his remark about not being surprised that I had believed the student. The student was alive, I was alive, Richard was dead. It was pretty unambiguous.

I returned to campus after the so-called summer holiday – and after lockdown – in a state of mild and slightly vague anxiety. There were big signs in town saying WELCOME BACK. Even one or two on campus. If I had been nervous about seeing colleagues in the flesh, rather than on my laptop screen, I needn't have been. In our shared office the first day I went back I found Will, Cath and Jonathan. Our new shared office, I should say. We'd been moved from the first to the fourth floor.

I might have to start getting the lift, I said. I'm out of breath.

Doesn't bother me, Will said and laughed – and Cath and I both laughed along with him.

Will was dead and had been dead when he'd joined the department five years ago. I remembered giving him lots of advice, standard advice you give a new colleague, and he hadn't taken any of it the wrong way. Cath – and Will – had joined the department too recently to remember when summer holidays were just that, before the change to workloads that saw us having to continue with supervision over the summer, but Jonathan was a veteran, like me.

Jonathan, I said, did you have a good holiday?

Holiday, he said, what holiday?

The door opened and Simon came in. The new office, as well as being on a higher floor, was bigger than the old office and Simon's desk was right over the other side from mine, which was perhaps why he didn't respond when I called out a greeting to him. Simon had been around almost as long as me and we got on. He was funny. He was dead as well. Or, as Maeve might say, formerly living.

I couldn't stop thinking about Richard, so I went and knocked on Ravi's door.

Sorry to unload on you on the first day back, I said – and proceeded to unload, which involved retelling the whole story, having a bit of a moan about Maeve and making the point that it would have been nice to have heard about Richard's appointment from someone in management rather than by Chinese whispers.

Ravi asked me if I had read much around the subject. There's a lot of very helpful literature to help with education and sensitivity, he said. I could definitely give you a reading list.

I don't want to read around the subject, I said. I don't think I need a reading list. I simply asked a colleague – in fact, I didn't ask him, I asked him how he might *feel* about apologising to a student. I didn't *tell* him to do it or *ask* him to do it. I asked him how he might *feel* about doing it.

You know, he said, you have to think about how what you say is going to be received by who you say it to.

I do that automatically, I said, with everyone. I always think about how what I say is going to be received by who I say it to. That's just normal. Everyone does that. Don't they?

Ravi gave me what I thought was meant to be a sympathetic smile. I had hoped for a sympathetic ear.

Richard was upset, he said.

I'm sorry Richard was upset, I said. I was upset too. I still am. Do you know what he said to me in an email? He said, I see you believed the student. That's not surprising. He was basically accusing me of being deathist, but was careful not to use the word.

You have to think about how what you say, he said, again, will be received by who you say it to.

You said at the time, in an email, that it seemed like I'd done all the right things, I said. You even thanked me for my diplomacy. Richard upset a student, I said, and gave him some unhelpful advice. There are publishers actively looking for specifically the kind of stuff the student was writing. Surely it's my job as module leader to point that out, to deal with the situation?

Ravi gave me the smile again.

By your reasoning – and Maeve's reasoning – if I can't point out where a dead colleague is going wrong, if I can't give them advice regarding how to do the job, I said, I shouldn't really be in a supervisory role over them, would you agree? So, what do you think? Can a dead person never have a living manager?

Ravi and I each held our gaze and then I looked away.

This is doing my head in, I said, having this hanging over me. What if I were to apologise to Richard for upsetting him. Would that make it go away?

I couldn't believe what I had heard myself say.

I think if you were to apologise to Richard, Ravi said, you would be doing it for yourself.

I can't win, I said.

Why, Ravi said, does it have to be about winning?

I give up, I said. Thanks for your time.

I headed back to the shared office. Two or three colleagues who worked with Simon on his side of things were gathered around his desk. They looked up and fell silent as I walked across the office. Cath and Will and Jonathan had all disappeared; perhaps they were teaching. I sat at my desk and looked out of the window. The view was an improvement on the view from the old office; there was that. Simon and the others got up and moved towards the door. As they left the room, Simon cast a brief look back at me. Then the door closed behind them and I was left alone.

Safe

It was the first flat she'd looked at, so maybe she wasn't ready for it. Plus it was unusual. Unusual in just about every way. Maybe unusual was good. She didn't know yet, didn't have anything to judge against. She just knew she needed to move. And fast.

There were more than thirty flats in the building, but only half as many parking spaces. It didn't matter; she didn't drive. Her ex had been the driver. The flat had two bedrooms, tick. Top floor, tick. But then the combined kitchen/living room. She wasn't sure about that. And the fire escape thing, she wasn't sure about that either. And then, of course, there was what had been left in one of the bedrooms. How would she get rid of that? She couldn't even move it.

It's the first flat I look at that I really like, and I really do like it. Two bed, top floor, perfect. Outside space, even better. The kitchen/reception room – OK, I can work with that. Isn't that the way most flats are these days anyway? You walk past those ground-floor conversions in West Didsbury and all those big front rooms are filled with islands and extractor hoods and people standing round with glasses of cava. Or are we back on to prosecco now? Whatever.

This will definitely do for me, even if I'm slightly puzzled by the safe.

The agent was hovering, as they do. Why do they insist on showing you round? This is bedroom one, this is bedroom two. This is the kitchen-diner and living area. Why won't they just let you look round on your own? You can almost certainly distinguish a bedroom from a reception room. The private roof space is all yours, he says. What about this door, you ask. That's probably the fire escape, he says. Probably? If you're going to show someone round, at least get your story straight, get all the information, be able to answer my questions, you think to yourself. So does that mean I'd have people walking across my private roof space, you ask him. Er, I guess so, he says. You guess so? How is it private in that case? Is that why there are bars on the windows despite it being on the top floor? Maybe you could remove them, he suggests. You're not sure he really gets it. What about this thing, you ask him when you're back inside. The safe, he asks. Yes, this great big bloody safe. Is it staying or going? I could ask the owner for you. It would be good to know, so maybe, yeah, ask the owner, 'cause, you know – you say, trying and failing to move it even an inch across the bare floorboards – it doesn't feel like it's going anywhere.

The agent looked apologetic, slightly dejected in a round-shouldered, stooped sort of way. He also looked about fifteen.

'I'm sorry,' he said. 'None of my female colleagues were available?'

Was available, she thought to herself, but didn't say. She got the feeling he understood, though, even if the agency didn't. He stayed as far away from her as he possibly could while still remaining in the flat.

'Can you tell me about this?' she asked him.

'It looks like a safe?' he said, every statement a question.

'I know,' she said. 'But why is it still here? There's nothing else in the flat. Just this safe. What would I do with it?'

He looked at it for a moment, then his eyes widened and he looked up at her.

'Cool table?' he said. 'Or bedside thing?'

'Bedside thing?' She was being cruel. He was doing his best.

He shrugged and looked at the window, then back at her.

'That's a nice cardigan,' he said and then vertical frown lines appeared above his nose. 'What colour would you say it is?'

'Um, red?' she said, pulling its long sides around her hips.

'I thought it might be scarlet or something,' he said, touching his nose.

'Has anyone put in an offer?' she asked.

As soon as she sees it, she wants it. Not the flat, the safe. The flat has a few problems. The funny kitchen/reception room. Won't her books get all greasy and damp and start smelling of onions and garlic? The terrace. She'd love some outside space – a balcony or a private terrace – but this roof-cum-fire escape, she's not sure about that. She doesn't want a certain someone using it in reverse to come and pay her a visit. But she thinks she can live with that risk for this. This old safe. About three feet high. Three feet square. Three feet cubed, in fact. Like the last shot of a low-budget remake of *2001: A Space Odyssey*. The empty flat and the big black safe. It's locked, of course.

She wants the agent to go away. She wants the next three weeks gone. She wants to buy the flat and move in without delay. She can hear the agent in one of the other rooms. She kneels down next to the safe and puts her cheek against the cool metal. She places her ear against the door and turns the dial. It clicks, like in the films. She would never need to go out.

I offered over the asking price. I had to have it and I had the money, from the divorce. I wasn't worried about the fire escape. I had the bars on the windows. I doubted the fire escape had ever been used, in any case, either the route across the roof or the metal steps that descended three floors to the communal gardens.

I didn't have a lot of stuff to move in. That wasn't what it was about. I unpacked some kitchen things, a box of books. My clothes. I had my bed in one bedroom and the safe in the other. I sat on the floor next to it and spun the dial, listening to the faint clicks.

I never had any contact with the vendor, having dealt only with the agents. I didn't ask them if they had the combination because I didn't want them contacting the vendor and asking him. It wasn't on the list of fixtures and fittings. I would find a way to open it at some point. It didn't matter how hard it was to get into it, how many cups of tea it took, how many false starts I made. I'd be like the screenwriter with the typewriter and the overflowing waste basket of discarded beginnings, each one a different way into the story. But I'd get there in the end.

We pass in front of the building, leaving it to our right, and enter the communal gardens. We cross the grass, heading towards the black metal steps. Up these we go, one storey, two, three. At the top we move across the roof to the east-facing exterior wall. The barred window reveals a basic kitchen. There are shelves with tins and jars on and space left to be filled. A large cardboard box sits on the floor, open at the top, the name of a removals firm printed on the side. The kitchen extends back into a living area. Moving to the right, we turn left, staying close to the north-facing wall. The first window reveals a bed, made up, in a room that's otherwise bare apart from another brown box, this one still taped shut. We glide forward to the next window. Getting up close, between the bars, we see a solid-looking old-fashioned black safe sitting on the floor in the middle of the room. Nothing else is in the room, except an unwashed empty mug on the floor.

There is nothing on top of the safe. On the safe door, which is closed, there is a dial and a handle. At the bottom, sticking out from the narrow gap between safe and safe door, is a small, red, woollen triangle.

The Child

The light was just beginning to fade when I found the shop.

I'd been wandering around the so-called Northern Quarter for much of the afternoon. When I last lived in Manchester, in the 1970s, the Northern Quarter didn't exist. It was a grey area between Shude Hill and Ancoats then. A post-industrial hinterland of broken windows and empty warehouses. Tib Street was full of pet shops; it smelled like a hamster's cage. There was the odd record shop, perhaps, but nothing much going on. I left for London in 1982 and didn't start coming back until the 90s. I had no reason to visit Oldham Street or anywhere else in the Northern Quarter, as the area started to become known towards the end of that decade. Businesses opened in refurbished buildings, the odd café or bar. Crafts places, wholefood. By the middle of the 'noughties', when I moved back, the area had changed a fair bit.

I was looking for places I recognised. It was either that or get on with decorating the spare room, as I had friends coming at the weekend.

The smells of straw and pet food had drifted away from Tib Street. The new boutiques that had sprung up were filled either with urban streetwear that didn't seem quite me, or with stuff

I'd owned in the 1970s: sheepskin-lined denim jackets, plastic Adidas kit bags, parkas with fake-fur trim. The bookshops on Shude Hill didn't have the allure they'd once possessed. The guys behind the counter were probably the same blokes from twenty-five years earlier. They were certainly wearing the same clothes, and didn't look like they'd washed them.

I was about to head back to my flat in Whalley Range when I spotted a window deep in shade on the wrong side of Lever Street. A line of videos, couple of DVDs. *The Texas Chain Saw Massacre*. Hitchcock's *Frenzy*. *Emmanuelle*. A naked bulb could be seen burning inside. Low wattage. I tried the door, descended a flight of steps. My nostrils flared at the damp and something else, an animal smell. Out of the gloom came a flash of white teeth, a glistening tongue. I leapt backwards.

'Baz, sit!' said a voice from somewhere.

The Alsatian sat back on its haunches, meek as anything.

'Sorry, mate.'

The speaker was a tall dark-haired man in his early twenties. He unfolded his insectile body from the stool where he'd been sitting behind an antediluvian cash register and stood, albeit with a pronounced stoop on account of the low ceiling.

'Stay, Baz,' he said to the dog, then looked at me. 'Are you looking for anything in particular?'

His polite manner was a surprise. I stared blankly at a shelf of exploitation films, only half-familiar with the titles.

'Just browsing,' I said.

'Let me know if I can help,' he offered, returning to his stool and picking up a smouldering cigarette.

I looked around. He had an interesting if limited selection. There was an attempt at categorisation but it was no more rigid than his shelving system and certain titles had ended up in the wrong place. Different formats – VHS, DVD – were mixed in together. Apart from a torn *Pink Flamingos* poster, the walls were bare and cracked. Even with my enthusiasm for some of the stock, I found the place depressing.

'There's more stuff through there,' the young man said behind me.

I turned. He was pointing to a plastic-strip curtain hanging in a doorway.

'Your adult section?' I guessed.

'Kind of.' He stubbed out his cigarette and stood up again. Close to, he really was remarkably tall. I wanted to tell him to stay sitting: it would be kinder to his back. But he was already pushing aside the rainbow-coloured plastic strips. I followed him through. The smell back here was more pungent. The damp was eating away at the plaster, which was crumbling behind flaking paintwork. The decay felt like it might be contagious.

The back room did contain adult material, but not of the usual kind. Instead of videos labelled *Playboy* or *Electric Blue*, I found stacks of Russ Meyer films and quasi-innocent 70s softcore of the type once screened constantly on Channel 5. Lesbian vampire flicks. *Confessions* movies. Dropped in among the dross were more mainstream films with notable erotic content: *Bad Timing*, *Daughters of Darkness*, *The Draughtsman's Contract*. I flicked through the Russ Meyer titles. These were the kind of films I'd had to leave Manchester to find. Sex scenes I'd seen on TV as a boy had been witnessed in clenched embarrassment as my mother fiddled with the pleats of her skirt and my father tutted loudly enough to be heard over the soundtrack. I rarely got to see films on my own, but when I did, by sneaking downstairs after my mother had gone to bed and my father was on a night shift, and I was lucky enough to catch something worthwhile, it meant all the more. I stored up fleeting glimpses of nudity. Cybill Shepherd's shy disrobing, watched by awestruck admirers, in *The Last Picture Show*. Diana Dors and Erica Beer, separately, trying and failing to seduce a much younger John Moulder Brown in *Deep End*. Such scenes had awakened in me a sense of wonder coupled with an equally potent sense of guilt. After staying up late to watch *The Vampire Lovers*, I checked the hamster's cage as part of my routine before sneaking back up to bed. The hamster was lying very still in the wrong part of the cage. I took it out and it felt different in my hand, cold and heavy. I put it back and the following day had to pretend that I hadn't known. Overcompensating, I insisted on burying the remains in the garden. At the back of one of the flower beds, past the remains of my father's latest bonfire, I knelt down and dug a little hole with the trowel, then pressed the body of the hamster as deep into the soil as it would go. For some time I felt uncomfortably guilty about having left the hamster lying dead in its cage overnight.

My illicit late-night screenings were undoubtedly what led to my becoming a film journalist. I went to London to go to university, then narrowly avoided getting thrown off the course for never showing up. When I wasn't in a Wardour Street preview theatre or catching up on lost sleep after an all-nighter at the Scala in King's Cross, I was ensconced in the college newspaper office in the union building writing up film reviews on a golfball typewriter.

'Some of this stuff's pretty rare,' the young guy said. He had taken a few videos off a shelf and was blowing the dust off them. The title of one of them caught my eye and it was like spotting the twinkle of gold in a prospector's pan.

Thundercrack!

I'd seen it only once, at the Scala, as part of a double bill. The other half of the programme had been wiped from my memory.

That was the effect of *Thundercrack!*, the most outrageous and depraved film I'd ever seen. It was also funny, weird and oddly erotic. I knew people who swore by the love scene in *Don't Look Now*. Others who got off on *Ai No Corrida*. I even had a friend who said he'd sat through Cronenberg's *Crash* in a 90-minute state of arousal. Maybe they had never seen *Thundercrack!*

'I didn't know this was available,' I said.

'It's not,' said the tall guy, with a little smile. 'Have you ever seen it?'

I told him about the Scala. 'You're too young probably even to have heard about it,' I added.

'My dad used to screen *Thundercrack!* in Manchester in the 80s,' he said. 'My name's Joe, by the way. Joe Hoffman.'

We shook hands. I told him my name.

'Your dad wasn't…' I began.

'Anthony Hoffman, yeah.'

Anthony Hoffman had been a face on the Manchester scene in the 80s. He'd known people at Granada TV and Factory Records and Savoy Books and so on, and was often seen at the same parties as Tony Wilson or David Britton.

'How's he doing these days?' I asked.

'Not so good.'

Unsure what to say, I looked at the photocopied notes on the back of the video box.

'So he used to screen this?' I said, eventually.

'Yeah, he'd hire a 16mm print and book a little back room somewhere. Word would get out and the place would be rammed. He even rented the Apollo once or twice.'

'I had no idea,' I said.

The Apollo had been where I'd gone to gigs. I tried to imagine this guy's father hiring it for a film screening. *Thundercrack!* was directed in 1975 by Curt McDowell and written by

McDowell in collaboration with underground film-maker George Kuchar. A group of characters are forced to spend the night in a big old house where they have sex with each other in a variety of different ways and permutations. As Kim Newman writes in *Nightmare Movies*, 'The film is too doom haunted to appeal to a gay or straight porno audience, and yet its two hours plus of penetrations, perversions and come-shots make it all but unbearable for anybody else.'

Some would disagree.

'The number of times his screenings were raided by the police,' Joe said. 'Ironic, really.'

'Why ironic?' I asked, a bit too quickly.

His only response was to light another cigarette.

'The 80s were James Anderton's heyday,' I remarked.

'Yeah. I don't know how many prints of *Thundercrack!* his lot must have ended up with. My dad told me he never got them back.'

'Maybe they burned them?' I suggested, remembering the frequent bonfires my father lit in our back garden.

'Yeah, maybe.' Joe prodded a patch of loose plaster on the wall with one of his Converse baseball boots. It fell off and a large spider scuttled away. 'I think he was deliberately trying to wind the police up – and succeeding.'

'Wouldn't have been difficult,' I said. Not with the chief constable being a self-declared born-again Christian. Although I'd been living in London at the time, I'd been aware of Anderton's increasingly bizarre pronouncements. It was hard not to be, given what my father did for a living. The mid 80s were strange times. On the one hand you had Nicolas Roeg, co-director of the splendidly amoral *Performance*, making TV ads warning of the danger of AIDS, and on the other there was James Anderton, God's copper, suggesting that people with

AIDS were 'swirling around in a human cesspit of their own making'.

'I gather he lives in Sale with his wife now,' Joe said. 'Does a lot of charity work. I imagine he's doing better than my dad anyway, who lives in a nursing home in Old Trafford. Sits there staring out of the window. On one side of the building you've got a park full of dogshit, pissheads and other assorted miserable cunts, and on the other you've got Old Trafford. My dad's a lifelong Blue.'

He stared at me with anger in his eyes. I held his gaze for a moment, thinking of my own father.

'How much is this?' I asked him.

'Ten quid, mate.'

As we left the back room I noticed another open doorway on the other side of the shop.

'This place goes on for ever,' I said.

'I've got more space than I can fill, and more than I can afford, more to the point. I'm looking to sublet that side. Dead cheap. Fifty quid a week. Sixty tops. If you know anyone…'

'It's tempting,' I said, before I could stop myself.

'Really? What would you sell?'

'Nothing. I'm thinking of starting up a little magazine. A film magazine. Something small, subsidised.'

'Cool.'

'I don't suppose I'll do it,' I said, waving my hands as if I could waft the idea away. 'I wrote some pieces for *8020*, which folded. I approached *City Life*, about doing some film stuff for them, the week before the *Guardian* closed them down.'

'Do you write for anyone else?'

'I write for the nationals and *Sight & Sound*, but I wanted to do something locally. I grew up here and I've moved back. I want to belong again. Do you know what I mean?'

'Yeah, yeah.' He nodded, reaching for another fag.

I handed him a tenner for the video and he started hunting around for a bag.

'It's all right,' I said.

As he passed me the video he said, 'Think about the space. I could let you have it for fifty.'

I smiled. 'Nice talking to you,' I said, and moved towards the steps up to the door.

'Wait,' he said, rummaging around in a drawer.

He came over to me with a DVD in an unmarked case.

'Have a look at that,' he said, pressing it into my hands.

I asked him what it was.

'Something my dad shot. I think you'll find it interesting.'

'OK,' I said. 'How much do you want for it?'

'Nothing. Borrow it. Watch it and bob back with it at some point. There's no hurry.' He smiled uncertainly. 'Keep it to yourself, though.'

I promised that I would, then turned my back on him and climbed the stairs to the street. I looked back through the window and saw him bending down to give the dog a stroke or a pat or whatever it is people give dogs.

I headed back to the multistorey where I'd parked the car. Leave the ground in Manchester and you can see the hills. I unlocked the car, but instead of getting in I wandered over to the concrete balustrade and looked out over east Manchester at the mountains in the distance, only ten or fifteen miles away. The snow that had fallen a week earlier glowed in the twilight.

My father had often taken me walking in the Peaks at weekends, when he wasn't working. He did shift work. He was a copper. He worked for Chief Constable James Anderton.

*

34

When I got back to the flat, I had a bite to eat, then installed myself in front of the TV with a beer, and slipped *Thundercrack!* into the VCR. I was only ten minutes into it when the phone went.

The machine answered and as soon as I heard Simone's voice, I hurriedly picked up the remote and switched off the TV. The sound of Simone's voice still managed to make me feel guilty about watching something like *Thundercrack!* Without her being in the room. Without even being in the same city. Simone was one of the reasons why I left London. And why I would never go back. Not until I knew she was either safely attached to someone else or living in another country.

There was nothing much to her message. Could I call her when I got a chance? But I knew that if I picked up the phone I'd get the same old questions.

I stopped the tape. I couldn't watch it now, not with Simone's voice in my head. I picked up the unmarked DVD-R that Joe Hoffman had lent me. I put it in the machine but it wouldn't play. Nothing doing, no menu screen or anything. I tried it in my laptop with the same result. Frustrated, I went to bed, thinking that I would take it back the next day. The fact that it wouldn't play naturally made me even more interested in finding out what was meant to be on it.

In the morning, however, I realised that finishing the spare bedroom had to take priority. Otherwise my guests wouldn't be able to move for wet paint. While I worked I daydreamed about the magazine I wanted to start up. As the hours went by and the walls got whiter, my plans acquired more depth and detail, but at the same time departed further and further from practical reality until I reached a point at which I acknowledged it simply wasn't going to happen. There would be no magazine and I wouldn't be renting Joe Hoffman's spare office space. But

I still needed to go back to his shop to query the DVD. When I finished painting, however, it was too late and the next day my friends arrived from London.

We had a good weekend; a lot of food and drink was consumed. They were my closest friends and it was good to see them again. I was gratified that they had come up so soon to see me in Manchester. It was the next week before I could get back to the shop on Lever Street, and when I did, I found the window bare and the door locked.

I pushed and pulled at the handle and knocked on the glass. I even got down on my hands and knees and called Joe's name through the letter box, but the shop was empty. No stock, no dog, no Joe. As I stepped back into the road and craned my neck to look at the upper storeys of the building, a police car cruised by. The driver slowed down; he and his colleague stared at me until I turned and walked away.

When the cop car had gone, I turned back. The shop had not had a name or a board outside and there weren't any other signs of life in the immediate vicinity. I walked around the block and tried in a couple of CD shops, but neither Joe's name nor my description of his shop rang any bells. I asked in Vinyl Exchange, where they sold videos and DVDs in the basement. Nice folk but no joy. I couldn't think where else to try. Shops like Joe's came and went and these days the trend was definitely towards closing down rather than opening up, even in the Northern Quarter.

I drove back through Hulme, which had changed more radically than the Northern Quarter in the years I'd been away. Gone were the concrete crescents and the Aaben Cinema, where I'd seen what I'd thought was the most outré cinema Manchester had had to offer in the early 80s. Fassbinder. Waters. Wenders. It was nice to think I'd been wrong, but frustrating not to have any way of finding out what was on that DVD.

I heard the yelp of a siren behind me and instinctively went to pull over to let them pass, but when I looked in the mirror I saw a police car with no intention of overtaking.

Apparently I'd been speeding. I protested that I couldn't have been doing more than 35 and I got the full sarcastic treatment. *Is this your car, sir? Do you know what the speed limit is, sir? Have you been drinking at all, sir?* I thought about mentioning my dad, but I could see from the officer's small, flat, joyless eyes that there was no point. At least he seemed to enjoy giving me a ticket.

When I got back behind the wheel, instead of turning left for Whalley Range, I kept going towards Old Trafford. Somewhere in this Escher diagram of pebble-dash council blocks and blood-redbrick terraced housing was Joe's dad, the legendary Anthony Hoffman, sitting staring into space – or at an empty park. I drove around for half an hour but succeeded only in making myself question the wisdom of having moved back to Manchester. How did I even know that Joe's description of the nursing home's location was accurate? There'd been something of the performer about him, as if he'd been sitting in his lair waiting for an audience to come along. Maybe he was a fantasist and not even related to Hoffman. Or maybe you had to ease yourself out of the nursing home window on a mechanical platform to glimpse either a patch of grass or the white Meccano exoskeleton of the football ground.

I gave up and drove home. At one point a police car seemed to be following me. Just as I was about to make an unnecessary left turn to make sure, it took a turning off to the right. In my rear-view mirror I saw the passenger's face at the side window. It was impossible to say whether he was looking at me or just watching the traffic.

That night I lay in bed unable to sleep as I tried to work out my next move. I was in the middle of formulating a surprisingly simple plan that I decided was bound to succeed when I fell asleep and in the morning could remember not even the slightest detail. I showered quickly and drove into town, parking close to the Apollo Theatre and walking to St Peter's Square. I'd reasoned that Central Library might be able to provide me with a list of care homes in Old Trafford, but when I got inside the reference section I started by looking up Anthony Hoffman in the newspaper catalogue. There was tons of stuff. The illegal screenings of *Thundercrack!* at the Apollo were mentioned. I flicked through bound copies of the *Evening News* and scanned the nationals on microfilm for more in-depth reports. One story in the *Guardian* listed the gear the police were supposed to have confiscated from Hoffman along with a 16mm copy of *Thundercrack!*, namely two 8mm movie cameras, a professional-standard 16mm Bolex and enough film stock to make a dozen full-length features. The article quoted an *Evening News* journalist, John Cavanagh, who claimed that Hoffman and his colleagues were legitimate film-makers, who, contrary to the story put out by the police, were embarked on a mission to clean up Manchester.

Intrigued by this, I looked up Cavanagh and found a whole bunch of references to pieces of his in the *Evening News* that suddenly stopped appearing around the time he was quoted in the *Guardian* story.

Cavanagh was easy to track down. He was in the book. There were a few listings under Cavanagh, J, so I went for the one in the most down-at-heel district and got lucky. He agreed to meet me and suggested Spearmint Rhino. I wasn't sure I could handle that, so he named a pub in Harpurhey I'd never heard of. When I got there, it was a strip joint, so I was vying with three naked girls for Cavanagh's attention. Their bellies were bigger than their boobs, but he didn't seem to mind.

'Call me Cav,' was all I could get out of him for the first ten minutes.

I went looking for the gents and had a bit of trouble finding it. The first door I tried down the darkened corridor that had been indicated led straight outside. Eventually I found it and stood staring at the cracked tiles wondering what on earth I was doing there. On my way back I got Cav another pint, determined that I would wring some information out of him.

You could tell he'd been a decent-looking young man, but had let himself go quite badly. Pouch-like bags under his eyes, grubby shirt buttoned tightly over a drinker's paunch. The girls left the stage for a minute and I pressed him. He'd not written for the paper, he confirmed, since being quoted in the *Guardian*.

'Someone told me,' he said eventually, 'that Hoffman had other stuff confiscated, stuff that was never reported. Films he'd shot on Super 8 at parties in south Manchester. Powerful types, you know. Councillors, magistrates, justices of the peace.'

'Did he ever show this stuff?' I asked him.

'That's unconfirmed.'

'The police had a particular incentive to keep those films out of circulation, then?'

Cav shrugged, then brightened as the girls reappeared.

'Where's Hoffman now?' I asked.

'Some home near Old Trafford.'

'Name?'

His fingers were splayed on his stained jeans as he watched the routine.

I took a twenty out of my wallet and folded it into his hand.

He told me a name and the next second there was a commotion from the bar area. I heard someone shout 'Police!' and I leapt from my seat and ran to the darkened corridor, where I pushed open the door to the car park. I didn't look back as I ran.

Driving back into town, I took the DVD-R out of my inside pocket and looked at it. The purple underside reflected a rainbow of colours that reminded me of the curtain in Joe's shop. As I waited for the lights to change at the bottom of Cheetham Hill, I wondered if this simple plastic disc was worth all the trouble I was getting into. Then, as a police car pulled silently alongside and I felt my heart rate quicken, I thought about what might be on the disc and why Joe had given it to me. Perhaps because I'd told him I wrote for the papers. It took all the self-control I had not to turn and check out the uniforms in the next lane. I couldn't be sure which cops were after me and which were not. The lights changed and they veered off to the right. I went the other way.

It turned out the place in Old Trafford where Hoffman was holed up was a lot closer to the park than it was to the football ground. It also turned out that there was a dark blue Cavalier parked outside the front entrance with three burly-looking plainclothes men sitting inside it. Still fifty yards away, I backed up and turned around. Admittedly, performing this manoeuvre was tantamount to winding my window down and shouting 'Come and get me, coppers', but it was marginally less risky than carrying on and driving right past them. As far as I could tell, no one followed me back to Chester Road. At the Chorlton turn-off I thought about going straight on to Sale, but resisted that temptation and turned left, heading for home.

I parked two streets away and approached on foot. There was no car outside, and the door hadn't been forced. I climbed the stairs and everything seemed normal. Surely I was being paranoid. The raid on the strip joint was routine and I'd got a ticket for driving in excess of the speed limit. Simple as that.

I unlocked the door to my flat and saw that it wasn't, in fact, as simple as that.

The place had been turned over. Looking at it with cold detachment, which I found I could do, in a looking-down-from-above sort of way, what they had done was quite impressive. Every movable surface was at a new angle to all others. Upended cupboards, overturned drawers. The mattress had been slit open with a knife, pillows eviscerated. Every book or CD or DVD or video that had been on a shelf was now on the floor creating a restless sea of plastic and paper. I was reminded of the Paul Nash painting of downed German warplanes in a Cowley field, *Totes Meer*.

There was a smell in the flat, too, that reminded me of Joe Hoffman's shop. It wasn't damp. It was the animal smell. They had come with dogs.

The TV, DVD player, VCR and my computer were gone, as if to make me think I'd been burgled, yet they'd left no signs of forced entry. It was this detail that made me realise they were laughing at me.

I left the flat without bothering to lock the door and walked the long way around to where I'd parked the car. I felt dissociated from reality as I drove over to Sale. James Anderton wasn't the only ex-Manchester copper who'd retired there. I parked across the road from my father's semi, its dimensions presumably much less generous than those of Anderton's place, wherever that was, perhaps on The Avenue or somewhere like that. I tried to imagine crossing the road and walking up the path. Knocking on the door. But I knew it wasn't going to happen. I was curious, though. I wondered if my dad had a DVD player, or maybe an old projector and a little pile of film cans. I wondered what went on behind those artificially leaded windows. I fingered the contents of my inside pocket and started the car engine. The house grew smaller in my rear-view mirror and I rejoined Washway Road, then slipped on to the M60, heading in an anticlockwise direction. Turning the clock back, I thought. Ha ha. It was getting towards rush hour, but the traffic moved smoothly enough. I got off on to the M67 and was held up in a long queue to join the road to Glossop. At the Glossop turn-off, I kept going, through Hollingworth and Tintwistle. The first of the reservoirs appeared below me to the right. At Crowden I pulled off the road and drove in a semi-circle to reach the car park.

The first paths were easy, nothing more than gentle diagonals up the side of the hill. I soon left the path and struck out for the quarry. There are two quarries at Crowden: a small one at the back of the hill only halfway up it, and a much larger one right at the top. It was the latter I was making for and once I had negotiated the scree slope I found myself having to grab handfuls of springy grass to help pull myself up a near vertical section. I was breathing heavily, but the tension that had knotted my muscles in the car while still in Manchester was easing. I could feel my heart beating as fast as a child's. Suddenly into my mind came the first X films I'd snuck into at the cinema, a double bill of David Cronenberg's *Shivers* and *Rabid* at the only picture house there had been in Altrincham in the 1970s. The slope above me began to level out or, more accurately, I could see nothing beyond where it stopped, so I knew I was near the top. The first film I could remember my parents taking me to was *Kes*. I remembered the contrast between the sense of freedom in the long shots of the kestrel's free flight and the stark finality of the shallow grave.

I pulled myself over the last ridge and dropped down into the scoured basin of the quarry.

My father had brought me here several times and no matter how much tension there was between us, it all fell away in the hush of the quarry, the towering gritstone bluffs like the walls of a ruined cathedral. The enormous static boulders. A very particular quality of stillness. As if this was a place in which man and nature had reached some kind of settlement. I climbed up the far side and walked up on to the moor. I turned for a moment and looked to the west, towards Manchester. I felt fully removed from the city and everyone in it. Turning my back, I considered the moor. In the distance was a trig point, beyond that and to the right the radio transmitter at Black Hill, where my father had taken me bog-trotting. I began walking. The going was soft – peat, heather, tussocky grass – but I covered a lot of ground. I walked hard for ten or fifteen minutes. I started to run. I felt free. Slowly the radio transmitter slid around to the left in relation to the trig point. When the two were aligned, I stopped, panting for breath, and knelt down. I took the DVD out of my inside pocket, still inside its clear plastic wallet, and inserted it into the damp, peaty earth, which accepted it as easily and smoothly as if it were a machine designed for that very purpose.

When I looked up I saw a pair of peregrine falcons in the distance, soaring and swooping over the quarry.

Full on Night

I turn the volume up as the front wheels make contact with the tarmac and the rear of the car leaves the driveway. The road is lit at regular intervals, the houses of our neighbours standing in darkness. Speed bumps force me to stay in low gear until I reach the main road where I signal to go right. A bus passes the stop on the other side of the road, empty but for a single passenger on the top deck. His silhouetted head narrows as he turns to look at the car nosing out of the side road.

I follow the bus, making no attempt to overtake. At the lights it goes straight on while I turn sharply to the left, enjoying the pull of the car towards the front off-side. The road surface is made up of flat blocks of orange broken up with lines of reflective white. The street lights are topped with misty coronas like dandelion clocks. The next set of lights changes to red as I approach and I knock the gear stick into neutral, allowing the car to coast. Another car sits at the adjacent stop line waiting to go, the driver's face ghostly in the glow of the dash. The traffic lights change in his favour and he moves forward.

I go on through one more set of lights and turn left into Burton Road. The restaurants and bars that earn this district its reputation are all closed. I slow down as I approach

Somerfield, indicate left and pull into the car park behind the shuttered supermarket.

There's one car parked behind the store itself, another two at the other end by the recycling bins. I roll down towards them and back up into a space a few yards short, switching off the engine. The CD, playing 'Full on Night' by Rachel's, stops as I do so.

I peer into the darkness – the car park is unlit – and pull down the stalk to activate my right indicator. Its rhythmic clicking is the only sound to be heard apart from the hum of traffic on the Parkway, even at this hour. After a couple of minutes I start the engine and a dissonant guitar riff accompanies my rolling the car back out on to Burton Road, then turning right into Nell Lane and heading for the Parkway.

Traffic on the motorway is light. I take the exit for Cheadle Royal and the patient piano work of Rachel Grimes ticks off the lighting poles on the wide loop around the back of the former Barnes Hospital and nearby disused Cheadle Bleach Works. The frantically bowed viola towards the end of 'Full on Night' is a suitable accompaniment to the scratching of the tree tops at the purply-orange sky.

I take the third exit off the roundabout at Cheadle Royal, skirting the miniature lake and heading deeper into the business park behind the sports and leisure centre. Behind an anonymous building of blond brick and green smoked glass I reverse into a parking space and sit and wait. The car park is divided by a line of low shrubs, beyond which two cars wait in darkness. In an hour or so, the first arrivals of the day will rumble overhead, travelling at a speed of 150 knots just 700 feet above the roof of the car. For now, though, all is quiet.

I turn the interior light on and let it burn for less than half a minute before switching it off again.

Nothing happens. No lights are lit in the other parked vehicles. No one approaches the car on foot.

I twist the key in the ignition and turn the wheel to drive down the other avenue on the far side of the island on the way out of the car park. The two cars, expensive saloons parked three spaces apart, appear empty, but the shallow angle of the windscreens makes it impossible to be sure.

I negotiate the roundabouts and head south on the Wilmslow road, turning right at the lights in the direction of Heald Green. A man in high-visibility clothing waits at a bus stop. A delivery van sits outside a convenience store, its rear doors folded back. I turn left into Styal Road and right into Ringway Road. I feel a slight tension as the Moss Nook restaurant appears and then retreats in the wing mirror. Moments later, on the right, there is a sudden break in the line of small, modest houses. On the other side of the road a bank of yellow-white approach lights marks the beginning of runway 24. I take the next road on the right and shortly afterwards another right turn into the Ringway Trading Estate. A light shines brightly on to the apron outside a depot on the left. I turn to the right and then go left in front of Air Freight Services. In the car park at the end, I turn around and back up to the chainlink fence.

I switch off the CD but keep the engine running and the lights on. Further down on the other side is a parked car. A dark shape is lodged in the driver's seat.

I reach down to kill the engine and extinguish the headlamps, then raise my hand to switch on the interior light and turn to you.

47

Simister

When Adam and Sara split up, he moved into a smaller house in Urmston, while she moved around the M60 to Simister. Sara got the cats and Adam got visiting rights, which he was happy should mean nothing more than feeding them when she went away. He knew it might be a bit of a trek, because, while it was only eight junctions on the motorway, he'd heard so many travel reports about 'the usual problems at Simister Island' that he didn't want to drive. Driving was a hassle. Sitting in traffic, or trying to find an alternative route, was a hassle. Sitting on a tram, even changing trams to complete a journey, was more than just preferable; it was a pleasure.

Sara was away for a week, with her new partner. Adam had had a new partner, but she had complained that he buried his feelings and he didn't have one any more. He had Barry instead. And he had work. But first he had to feed the cats and before that he had promised to visit Barry, or talk to the people looking after him. The hospital was literally at the end of the road.

'There's not much we can do,' a young woman staring at a device told him, 'apart from keeping him comfortable. And there's real pressure on beds.'

'Yes, you said.'

'And he's your uncle?' Her thumbs moved at speed over the device.

'No, I said he's *like* an uncle. He lives in my street. I look out for him—'

'We're not going to be able to keep him in much longer,' she said, cutting in, without looking up. 'Can I just check we've got your number?'

The Trafford Centre was a mile and a half away. He passed through the actual building as quickly as possible, but not quickly enough to catch the tram he watched pulling slowly away from the stop. Another arrived in a few minutes and Adam boarded. *This is a service to Cornbrook. The next stop will be Barton Dock Road.* If he ever fell in love again, it would be with the woman who did the announcements on the trams. Her voice was like a brew in a china mug on a cold morning. He didn't know where precisely her accent was from, but it couldn't be more than five miles from Piccadilly Gardens. He didn't know what she looked like, but when he heard her voice he pictured a forty-something blonde in a denim skirt who had served him once at the Apple Store.

He changed at Cornbrook. *This is a service to Bury. The next stop will be Deansgate-Castlefield.* He watched as another passenger noticed, apparently for the first time, the life-size cardboard cut-out of a woman in the window of one of the fourth-floor flats on Water Street. The young man in the seat in front of Adam pointed it out to his girlfriend and they both laughed. *We are now approaching Deansgate-Castlefield, where you can change for National Rail and free buses around the city centre.*

At Prestwich, Adam got off and walked through long, snaking streets of suburban semis, then passed through a short alleyway and emerged on to a wider, straighter road with a school on one side and, eventually, fields on the other, and then fields on both sides. He passed under a sign saying 'Welcome to Simister. Please Drive Carefully' and shortly afterwards there was a brief stretch of houses on both sides before these were replaced by the blue railings of a motorway bridge. He looked down at the traffic on the M60 moving surprisingly freely as it approached the huge roundabout that was the junction with the M62 and the M66. He was still glad he hadn't come by car. Once he was over the bridge the character of his surroundings changed subtly, unless he was imposing his own ideas on the nature of the neighbourhood, wondering whether the people in the houses on the other side of the motorway bridge regard- ed themselves as being equally *of* Simister. It was only after the motorway bridge that he spotted the first posters protesting against plans to build more than two thousand new homes, a new road and industrial units that would surround the village. 'BURY FOLK,' said the poster, Simister, like Prestwich, being part of Bury, 'KEEP IT GREEN.'

Sara's place was just past the Same Yet pub, she had said. He found the key under a plant pot, as she had told him he would. It was clearly that kind of place, at least until they built the two thousand new homes. The cats were both in the kitch- en. Adam paused by what he still regarded as his – or at least their – fridge-freezer, which reminded him he had to be home from work no later than six to take delivery of his replacement fridge-freezer. He quickly fed the cats. Jerry made an enthu- siastic start on his own bowl before he would no doubt go on to empty most of Margot's. The female, who was not a young animal, had lost her appetite and had been under investigation at the vet's, Sara had told Adam. No diagnosis had been made, but Sara had been warned to expect a swift decline. Adam took a picture of each of the two cats – Jerry still eating, Margot curled up on her folded blanket – and headed out.

He walked the same way back to Prestwich and boarded a tram to town. *This is a service to Piccadilly. The next stop will be Heaton Park.* He spent the day at work fine-tuning the presentations he had to give the following morning and the morning after, and was back home in Urmston before the opening of the window for delivery of the new fridge-freezer, which arrived an hour later within two minutes of the window closing, the driver complaining bitterly about the roadworks.

'Fibre-optic cables,' Adam told him as they stood outside his house looking at the barriers that completely blocked the road in one direction and made it almost impassable in the other. 'Still, you made it, and just inside the window.' He smiled.

The man didn't smile back, but went to his van and lowered the tailgate.

'Shall I help?' asked Adam.

'I can manage.'

It took a bit of effort to get through the door. Maybe if the man had been paying less attention to the contents of Adam's front room he would have accomplished his task sooner.

'Looking to Airbnb your front room?' the man said when he got the trolley into the hall.

'My wife and I split up,' Adam said. 'I got all the beds – we had three, for guests – and then I moved into a two-bed house…'

'She wanted a new one, eh?' the man said.

'I guess.'

In the kitchen the man grunted and Adam showed him where he wanted the appliance. A box-cutter appeared and the man removed the plastic and opened the box and adjusted the feet while Adam busied himself moving the packaging out of the way until it stood next to the door to the cellar. The man left, with Adam's wish that he have a lovely evening hanging in the air between them. Closing the front door, Adam could just make out the glare on the man's face as he glanced in the direction of the barriers.

The box and all the plastic went down into the cellar, where it stood next to Adam's share of the marriage's acquired gardening implements – a grass rake and a spade.

On the second day, Adam couldn't be late for work. Tony had been late when he had been due to give a presentation and look where Tony was now.

As Adam came out of the Trafford Centre, he saw a tram waiting at the stop. *This is a service to Cornbrook. The next stop will be Barton Dock Road.* He didn't even have to wait long at Cornbrook. *This is a service to Bury. The next stop will be Deansgate-Castlefield.* He looked for the cardboard woman. If anyone around him noticed her, they didn't react. From Prestwich he walked the same route. The suburban streets. The alley. The long straight road. The fields. Welcome to Simister. The outlying houses. The motorway bridge. The village proper. BURY FOLK. The Same Yet. He felt in his pocket for the key.

As he entered the kitchen, Adam saw Jerry coming towards him – and Margot curled up on the kitchen floor beyond him, but not curled up as she had been on her blanket the day before. He heard a voice say, 'Oh, no,' and took a moment to recognise it as his own. There was something subtly, yet distinctly – undoubtedly – different about Margot's appearance. Gingerly he touched her, picked her up. She felt like a stuffed animal. He quickly put her down again and checked the time. His schedule didn't allow for something like this.

He grabbed a food pouch and emptied the contents in Jerry's bowl. In a cupboard he found some plastic packaging, a label on it bearing Sara's name and new address. She would have had a top or a dress delivered in it. She had always been one for ordering things online (and trying them on and sending them back). He opened it up some more and spread it out on the floor, then picked up Margot's disturbingly lightweight body and placed it in the middle. He folded the corners over and then was uncomfortably aware of them flopping back into their original positions as he went to grab a roll of packing tape from the kitchen drawer. He bit off a length of tape and held it between his teeth while refolding the corners.

He put the secured package on Margot's blanket. Before leaving, he looked out of the window at the garden.

On the tram – *This is a service to Altrincham. The next stop will be Heaton Park* – he texted Sara and sent the picture of Margot he'd taken the day before. It was the last picture anyone would take of her, he explained, and added that he would go back later and bury her in the back garden, if Sara would like that. He remembered that when they had been married they had owned more than one spade, so, if he now owned one, Sara had to have the other. It was an elegantly simple, easily achievable solution. No hassle.

He was in the middle of his presentation when he felt Sara's response tickle his leg. He imagined the content of her message as he continued to run through his PowerPoint and make scripted jokes to colleagues. Would she approve his plan? Would she use emojis? There was a cat emoji, but was there a spade? He realised he was looking forward to burying the cat and so Sara's text, when he read it later, was a little disappointing. She had arranged with a vet's that she would deliver the body to the surgery and they would see that it was cremated. She sent him directions to the vet's, which, she said, was 'a bit out of the way'.

He left work early and got the tram – *This is a service to Bury.*

The next stop will be Victoria – back to Prestwich. Suburban streets, alley, long straight road, fields. Welcome to Simister. Houses. Motorway bridge. Village. BURY FOLK. Same Yet. He had started to become anxious in case Jerry might have interfered with Margot's plastic shroud, but the package was intact. He picked it up and immediately put it down again. The weight of it was still horribly wrong.

He left the kitchen, found the door to the cellar. There were lots of boxes, mostly too big, but he found one that, from its dimensions, might have contained a mirror or a toilet seat. He opened it on the kitchen floor and placed the package in the box – a perfect fit – and his fingers alighted on one unstuck end of tape. He thought about the vet's and how they might react. You wouldn't take a dead animal to the vet's in a plastic bag, which was basically what he was doing, but, on the other hand, when he thought about removing the tape and seeing the body again, he wasn't keen on this, so he closed the lid and picked up the box, keeping it flat, like a pizza.

He walked east on Simister Lane, as the village petered out. He soon realised there was no way he could carry the box pizza-style all the way to the vet's, so he tentatively turned it on its side, feeling the contents shift and settle. When he reached Blueball Lane, he took the turning. The road was narrow and deeply potholed, with fields on both sides. There was the constant noise of traffic from the M62 half a mile to his left. The road seemed to be going on for ever. Sara had not been joking: the vet's was more than a bit out of the way. Coming towards him was a man walking a dog.

'Am I going the right way for Heywood Old Road?' Adam said.

The man – sixties, heavyset, thick-framed glasses – stopped and his dog came bounding up to Adam, who moved the box to his other arm, away from the dog, but the dog ran behind him and jumped up at the box. The man told him the dog was only being friendly and Adam said it wasn't a problem, as he moved the box back to his other arm, and the dog simply followed wherever the box went.

'Heywood Old Road?' Adam asked.

'At the end of the road,' the man said.

'Great, thanks.'

The dog started barking at the box. The man opened his mouth to ask a question of his own, but Adam cut him off – 'Thanks for your help' – and marched off. The dog followed him for a bit before giving up. To Adam's right, across the fields, a white house had appeared in the distance. It seemed unusually tall and, with its two rectangular windows at the top and horizontal panel underneath them and single wide window underneath that, resembled a face. Some kind of modern, architect-designed house: who might live there, in the middle of a field, with the drone of the motorway to greet you whenever you opened a window? But the angles had been misleading. When Adam reached the main road, he found the white house to be situated not in a field but on the other side of Heywood Old Road and home to a firm of solicitors. The nose of the face had been the sign bearing the name of the firm.

He walked up Heywood Old Road for a few minutes and came upon the vet's. He entered and, seeing no one behind the counter, placed the box flat on the floor against the wall.

A woman in blue surgical scrubs appeared. Adam explained that his ex-wife had made an arrangement with the surgery and gave Sara's name. The woman turned to a computer.

'The name again?'

Adam repeated the name.

The woman shook her head, not looking up from the screen, and Adam pictured himself walking back down Blueball Lane with the box under his arm.

'The name of the cat?' the woman asked him.

Adam told her. She continued to search and to shake her head. Adam went through the sequence of events again and the woman relented.

'You can bring Margot in,' she said.

He gestured to the box on the floor.

'Ah,' said the woman.

Adam was halfway back to Simister when the hospital rang. The signal was poor, but he gathered that they were going to discharge Barry and that this seemed to require Adam's participation in some form.

'Seven—' the caller was saying.

'Pardon?' Adam said.

Silence, then: 'Can you be—?'

'Can I be what?'

'—seven p.m.?'

'Can I check you've got the right address for Barry?' Adam asked, but the call seemed to be over, whether ended by the other party or lost through the intermittent signal. Adam checked the time. It would be tight.

It was tight, but Adam made it home for seven, pleased with himself for having managed to pick up some supplies to go in his new fridge.

There was an ambulance parked outside his house. A driver stood waiting on the pavement with Barry semi-conscious in a wheelchair beside him.

'Hiya,' Adam said, to the driver. Was he a paramedic? He didn't look like a paramedic. He looked like a driver. 'Barry's place is just down there, actually.' He pointed.

'I'll never get past that lot,' the driver said, looking at the barriers. 'Anyway, this is the address I was given.'

'But he doesn't live here. He doesn't live with me. He lives at number fifty-two—'

'Looks like you're all set up, anyway,' the driver said, peering through the window. 'Bed downstairs. He can't be messing with stairs. Can we get this done? I've got another five patients to move yet. I've been on since eight this morning.' He was already wheeling Barry up the path.

'Whatever,' Adam said. 'I'll make him a brew and then *I'll* take him home.'

He got ahead of the man and unlocked the door.

'Give us a sec,' Adam said. 'I'll just dump this.' He indicated his bag of shopping. By the time he returned from the kitchen, the hall was empty. He found the pair in the front room, where the man had already unloaded Barry and somehow got him into bed. Barry's head lolled and his eyes were opening and closing.

'I'll make him a brew,' Adam said, heading back to the kitchen.

Returning to the hall he realised the driver had left, leaving the front door ajar. The ambulance went past the front of the house.

Adam took a mug of tea through to the front room and put it down on a bookcase next to the bed.

'How are you doing, Barry?' he said. 'Driver was nice, wasn't he?'

Barry looked at him without replying.

'Are you hungry, Barry?' Adam asked. 'I'll make you a butty. What do you like? Cheese? I'll make you a cheese butty.'

Ten minutes later, Adam took a cheese sandwich into Barry, who had fallen asleep, his tea untouched. Adam put the plate down next to the brew, left the room and closed the door.

In the morning, Adam went straight to the kitchen and made tea and toast – for two – and took Barry's into the front room, where he saw that his guest had touched neither his tea nor his sandwich from the night before. His head had slipped to one side on the pillow and his mouth had fallen open. Putting the tea and toast down on the bookcase, Adam stood by the side of the bed, watching Barry. He reached out a hand and touched Barry's arm and quickly withdrew his hand.

'Oh no,' he said.

He remained standing there for a minute, looking at Barry without really seeing him, as he ran through various scenarios, then he picked up the fresh tea and the plate of toast, leaving the cold tea and the sandwich, and returned to the kitchen. He poured the tea down the sink and put the toast down on the worktop next to his own toast. He took a bite from his own toast, and put it back down, then picked up a piece of Barry's toast and took a bite out of that. He drank some tea and continued to stand there looking at Barry's toast while his own toast and Barry's toast combined in his mouth.

He looked at his phone to check the time. He had to get over to Simister – he couldn't not feed Jerry – and then to work. He couldn't be late either.

He slipped the rest of the toast into the food waste caddy and poured the remains of his tea down the sink, then opened the door to the cellar and came back up to the kitchen with the polythene that had been wrapped around the box the fridge-freezer had come in. In the front room he spread this out over Barry's body. Then he picked up the cold tea and the cheese sandwich and left the room. He dropped the sandwich into the food waste caddy and poured the cold tea down the sink. He put all the dirty pots in the washing-up bowl, added a squirt of washing-up liquid and ran the hot tap until they were submerged. Returning to the front room and walking past the end of the bed without looking at Barry, he pulled the curtains to and left the room.

He walked to the Trafford Centre. *This is a service to Cornbrook. The next stop will be Barton Dock Road.* He changed at Cornbrook. *This is a service to Bury. The next stop will be Deansgate-Castlefield.* He looked out of the window in good time for the flats on Water Street. He briefly wondered if the woman in the denim skirt still worked at the Apple Store. He thought about Barry lying on the bed in his front room covered in plastic. *This is a service to Bury. The next stop will be Crumpsall. The next stop will be Bowker Vale. The next stop will be Heaton Park. The next stop will be Prestwich.* Suburbs, alley, road, fields, Simister, bridge, BURY FOLK, Same Yet.

He unlocked the door and was met by Jerry. Would Jerry need time to adjust to the absence of Margot? Would this feel different to Jerry than it had when Margot had gone missing for a week when Adam and Sara had still been together? Jerry appeared friendlier – or needier – than he often did to Adam, walking in and out of Adam's legs as they moved towards to the kitchen.

'I'm on a tight schedule or I would keep you company,' said Adam, as he tore open a food pouch. 'No, I would, really.'

The walk back to Prestwich. *This is a service to Piccadilly. The next stop will be Heaton Park... Abraham Moss... Shudehill.*

He made it in time for the presentation and once it was over he slumped at his desk. His colleague said a few of them were going out for a drink after work. Did he want to join them?

'I've got some stuff to take care of at home,' said Adam.

He walked to Cornbrook. *This is a service to the Trafford Centre. The next stop will be Pomona.* From the Trafford Centre he walked slowly, watching the light fade from the sky.

He brought the long box up from the cellar and stood it in the hall next to the door to the front room. Then he went to the kitchen and looked out of the window at the garden while washing up the breakfast pots. He thought about the alternatives. Call an ambulance? Why was Barry in his house? Because the driver insisted? Really? He was a miserable bastard, but did Adam want to get him into trouble? What if Adam somehow managed to get Barry down the road and into his own house? The alternatives had one thing in common: hassle.

He started taking off his rubber gloves, but then changed his mind and left them on.

Down in the cellar, he looked at the spade. He wondered if it was dark enough yet.

Disorder

The pain is back. Mine. More a sensation. You know, you re-member. Control the feeling, beware the fear. Change what you can control. Control what you can't change. In the end, all is lost.

Start again.

Where will you find a different way, the right road? It takes time. Make time your friend. Oh yeah, all that. I've run from friends and talked to strangers, and walked out of the city, far into the night. I tried moving, but only in my heart. I travelled far, but obtained nothing. She had everything. You had every-thing. Attracted to myths, you surrendered to angels. Searching for God's glow, you sank to the depths.

Start again.

I campaigned hard. I just didn't know what for. To get a feel-ing, to see your hand. Get lost, you said. But where? On my own or with you? I broke you, you said, clinging, directionless. Me, not you. Control. I had to keep control. For me, you filled a room. You were my world. I lost friends. I lost the centre. I lost my edge. The hopes I had tried to hold on to lay around me, kicking as they died. You showed me the world in a room. A cage, a lost childhood, the end of everything, the values of nothing.

Again.

Of the streets, of the houses, of the windows, of the door. Of the shadowplay on the wall. The feeling in my dreams, the spirit of my youth. The times. The times I've travelled and lost. The times I've screamed in the night. The time I've lost, waiting for something, waiting for someone, waiting for you. We were just bodies, you said, of blood and skins. Where was the spirit?

Christ, the tears I cried. The strangers I found and gave to you as toys. Their cold, wide eyes and thin faces. Their silence. To you it was bloodsport. Some died, many were lost and many more will not remember. They cried as they lay there. You turned to me. Oh, their tears. What did you want? The tears. The blood and the tears. We looked for too long. The sense broke down. They were just bodies, and so we took them to places of darkness and despair. Was this the end? Were we lost?

The change was hard and violent. You demanded a gun. She's gone, I thought. Lost. Occupied by death. Corrupted by sin. Where could we go? What could we do? Where was the way out?

We were living in a little room with wide cracks in one wall. The building's windows were dark all the time, the nights long, each day the same. A lost voice cried, in the distance, No, no, no. No more. Marked strangers walked in the roads, with eyes down. The city felt far away. All through those lost nights children screeched, regrets were distorted, and feeling lost out to noise and fire and pain. Friends-turned-judges took control and gave little away any more. Eyes flashing, cars crashing.

I've seized on mistakes and tried to get free. I've turned people into martyrs and pleasures into sadness. I've lost the means to connect, the will to know the truth. I've seen crowds die. I remember watching a man's violent end and not feeling it. Looking at a knife and not seeing power.

Much longer ago, in forgotten youth, I tried to control strangers and so made friends. These were fatal errors for me. I travelled by train through unknown territories without a guide and got lost. I looked in the eyes of assassins and something died. Where could I get control? Where could I find knowledge? It's a prophet you are looking for, a voice said. Where will I find one? Where, where, where? It's not where but when. So when? When you are close to the end. How will I know? All the disbelief and confusion will fall away. You will see long and wide. You will understand.

The body is weak. There's violent pain and a metallic taste. No control. Then no sensation, apart from all the rust and the thin odour of steel. There's no escape, no way out.

The bodies, in a row, move only when they are disturbed.

In the distance, through deep time, for me, childhood ends. For there's no more time and I'm no longer young. Not any more. Where is there now? What is there now? I'm afraid I've lost the stomach for it. I'm too weak, too far gone.

All right?

No, not really, I said.

I've been looking on, outside, watching through the window. I saw one passer-by, and a second. I saw four, ten, twelve. Is there no end to this? Where are they going on to, these strangers? Where and when will these trials end? No, let me guess.

In the car, getting out of the city. On a neon trail, lost time, enormous prisons for young sons long trapped, goaded by strangers. Violent eyes, wasted feeling, never worked, angry tears. Meet your end. I don't feel any more, just look and remember. You wanted to know, what did I see? A last chance, for them. Torn bodies grouped on the floor, again, in the corner.

Again.

Time to get out. We loaded the car and travelled slowly,

then faster, laughed as we were pulled over for our speed. Blue lights. Please step outside. For their eyes, for their fingers, for their bodies. For their control. For bloodsport. What a waste. To see the colours, to hear the sound, to feel the heat. To forget the moves and admire the spirit. To nail the feeling, to hold the sensation. To control the edge, to control the centre. To guess the end.

More bodies, for more control.

Will she lose interest? Can she keep secrets? The pressure is creeping up. I'm hoping, for me, it will all come to an end. The end of acting up, of looking lost, of moving on, of making do. What brought me here? What lies obtained my withdrawal from normal limits? Who were we in a different time? And from a different place? Where were we when, afraid, we tried to end it all? It's for her. It's for you. It's for her. It's for me. For mine. I've… I've seen friends share blame and strangers collect pity. I've set close friends (with habits, no saints) on the wrong way just to get some control. Different rules for strangers. A state of upheaval and a darker side. Forced tears, gaps in time, shown no clue. She's got her way. Again she's obtained control. She's trying a different line, she said. Soon we will know more. She will watch me and I will watch her. We'll each stare. It will all end and we will lose, again.

Pass me the phone… Hey. I— Yeah, sure. Yeah… Beside mine… No, too weak, too afraid… I get to meet too many… Where? Who by then? I've had mine for all of, well, since always… She may let me… Where were their—? Where now? … Right. Keep that. I know. That spirit… Damn it. His friend, the fence… Where? … When? Just a moment… Right. The tenth… Too wide and too frequent… Oh, where again? I think we're behind, though… Like, four sided, somehow… Special room for—? Use your senses to— Good. I had some in mine… There? Bed, sheets, floor. She had this place.

I'm told I guessed the right moment and you walked through the room. All that spirit and power and control. Until you lose it again, when you don't move any more, afraid of your own reaction, of looking lost.

She's distorted by drink, a waste. I saw it and walked away. The strain's getting too much. The end, within, the same but different. We'll take a chance. We've come this far and made some mistakes but obtained proof. Their ways are not a right any more. Beware a change, and a force, and a nature, and destroyed youth, and waste, and closed eyes and dancing, a waiting, a looking round, a knowing, a hoping, and wider, faster cars, the ocean getting warmer, dust, glory, inserted memory, style that's expressed with feeling, trying to take control, trying to lose control.

It gives way like low water. It takes control. It reflects on the past. It says, rise up. It slumps down. It means well.

I'm in shock. I saw it take some of me. I'm down there until I'm up here again. I've been afraid. I'll get better. I'll live.

You stare through me. I've had it with you. I made a move. Oh, I say, I did it again and I did it again and I did it again. I say, I don't know where this will end. Why can't I see it through to the end? She's guessed the right way. She's waiting again. She's obtained her own man. She's travelled on through time. She's filled with will. She's got to stop herself, got to close it, lose it. She's afraid she'd barely hold on.

You left around what time? To the nearest hour… But who with? Any more? … Where else? … The long way round… To who then? To another group? … To where? On this side?

… On that side… Shined lights at? … Yeah. Take your time… You saw your friend getting all cross? All right. Don't— Good. We don't care.

Keep control of new sensations. Act on urge in city centre. See portrait in plain style. Take stairs for pleasure. Descend by wire with own hand. Give control of motion to friend. Lose all feeling in hand. Think through new case. Treat fine lines in corner.

There were some leads long ago.

Shades of feeling seem to show more spirit.

Stay with the scene. Long takes. The spirit of the place. The feeling of the land. Wide view.

You saw all the red mess and edged through the room. I heard the chair upon the floor. You played your hand and I mine. We knew we had lost. Now I see the waste of it all. So many lost and some, who won't tell, still waiting. She'd had it all. In her way, did she care? Did she change?

I've talked for too long. But I've said it all. I have to live. Until there are no new sensations any more. Until the end.

The Dark Heart

Nick and Freya are in the living room sitting on the sofa. She is flicking through the films that he has recorded off the TV. She reads some of the titles off the screen.

'*Point Blank. Vertigo. Stalker. Down Terrace.* Have you not got any recent films?'

'*Down Terrace* was 2009,' Nick says.

'What's it about?'

'It's about criminals. One of them's a rat and they're trying to find out who.'

'Sounds great,' she says, deadpan.

'It's a comedy.'

'*Fight Club.* What's that about? *Rear Window.* What's *Rear Window* about?'

'It's about a man who watches his neighbours.'

'Creepy guy.'

'No, he's a nice guy. He—'

'Is it old?'

'Yes, it's old. More than fifty years old. Older than me.'

'That old?'

'Yes, that old. Do you want to watch it?'

Freya pulls a face. 'Ceebs.'

Nick picks up a cushion and throws it at Freya. She drops the remote and tucks the cushion under her legs, then picks up the remote again and switches back to live TV.

The kitchen is small enough that without either of them having to leave the table, Freya can get the orange juice from the fridge and Nick can get her a glass from out of the cupboard.

While the fridge door is open he looks at the bottles of strong Belgian beer he keeps in there.

'Do you want a beer, Dad?' she says. 'Go on. Have a beer.'

'No, thanks,' he says. 'Whose go is it?'

'Yours,' she says. 'No, mine.'

She rolls a double, puts him on the bar.

One of the phones buzzes against the table top. It's face up, which means it's his. He sees his mother's name and a text.

'Why do you have your mum listed in your address book under her name,' Freya asks, 'and not under Mum?'

'I don't know,' he says. 'Just that that's her name.'

'You're in mine as Dad,' she says.

'Right.'

'It's weird having her listed by her name. Why would you do that?'

He opens his palms. 'Seems normal to me.'

'What do you call her?' she says, insisting. 'You call her Mum. You don't call her Stella. You should change it.'

'OK, I'll change it,' he says. 'Whose go is it?'

Nick and Freya are playing backgammon in the kitchen.

It's a very small kitchen. The backgammon set takes up almost all of the small round wooden table that completely dominates the space. There's room, on one side of the table, for two mobile phones and the scorecard, while on either side of the board stand the two dice cups and two mugs of tea.

Freya, sixteen, has just started drinking tea.

Freya is ahead in the game, all the black counters, bar two, already in her home board. The scorecard tells its own story; Nick is ten games behind. Freya rolls a double four and moves her last two counters to safety.

'Now it's a race,' Nick says.

'Which you can't possibly win,' says Freya. 'Do you give up?'

Nick shakes his head. His hand closes around his mug, which he picks up and pretends to shake, as if it's his dice cup and he's about to throw his dice.

'Nooo, Dad!' says Freya.

He smiles and brings the mug to his mouth, then replaces it on the table and picks up the dice cup. He throws a one and a two.

'Nice throw,' Freya says. 'Now do you give up?'

'Go on then,' he says, picking up the dice and dropping them into his tea.

Nick switches the TV off and Freya gets up from where she has been sitting next to him on the sofa and says she's going to bed.

'Don't forget your teeth,' he says.

He watches the blank screen for a few moments then gets up and goes into the kitchen. The main light is off but the under-cupboard lighting is on. He hears Freya in the bathroom, cleaning her teeth. He opens the cupboard where he keeps the glasses and takes his binoculars down from the top shelf. He hears the bathroom light being switched off and Freya crossing the floor of the hall to her bedroom. He switches off the under-cupboard lighting and stands at the sink looking out of the window across the courtyard at the other flats. Not many lights are on.

'Nick?' Freya calls from her bedroom.

He turns away from the window. 'Yes?'

'Please will you bring me my charger?'

He puts the binoculars down on the worktop. The charger is on the coffee table in the living room. He knocks on her door and enters. She is in bed with the light off looking at her phone.

'Thanks, Nick.' She looks up, face lit by the screen.

He hesitates, gives a half-smile that she can't see.

In the kitchen he resumes his position at the sink and looks out into the night. There are lights on in only two of his neighbours' windows.

Nick and Freya are walking to the cemetery. It's late. The sun is setting, sky turning pink. They walk fast. She links his arm, then lets go. They pass the end of the road where her mum lives, where Freya lives, most of the time. They approach a pub. A man emerges, taking up the pavement, walking towards them, slightly unsteady. Nick and Freya move apart. The man grins, says, 'Hiya, mate,' and when he's gone, Freya links Nick's arm again.

'Do you know that man?' she says.

'No.'

'He seemed to know you.'

'Alcohol. It has a disinhibiting effect. Encourages you to say hello to complete strangers. As I imagine you probably know,' he says, looking sideways at her.

Freya smiles, lets go of his arm.

They cross the main road. The cemetery gates are closed but there's a gap in the railing.

'Can we get through there?' Freya asks.

'Easy,' Nick says.

They walk between the graves, find his dad's.

'It's grown a bit,' Freya says.

'A bit,' he agrees. 'Long way to go. I don't want my mum – your nana – to see this.'

He looks at the headstone, the lines of gilt lettering, the words, the dates. The large blank space underneath like a half-empty page waiting to be filled.

Nick tells Freya he's going for a walk and she asks where he's going. To the cemetery, he says. He tells her about his dad's grave, how the grass over the grave disappeared after they'd had a lot of rain and now it was just soil. He shows her a picture on his phone.

'The woman at the council said it had sunk or fallen in,' he says, 'because of the heavy rain.'

'Fallen in where?' Freya asks.

'I don't know,' he says, pulling a face.

He tells her how the woman at the council had said she would get it reseeded, but nothing had happened, so he'd been and scattered grass seed himself.

'I want to see if it's taken,' he says.

'I'll come with you,' she says. 'I fancy a walk.'

When he opens the door, he hears someone coming up the stairs. Freya steps out of the flat and he locks the door behind them.

'Hi, James,' he says to his landing neighbour, who has now reached the top of the stairs.

'Hi, Neil,' says the neighbour, glancing at Freya before unlocking his door and entering his flat.

Nick and Freya start walking down and when they've gone one flight Freya leans closer and whispers to him.

'Did he just call you Neil?'

'Yeah.'

Across from Nick's flat to the right, two floors down, a Black woman in a red dress stands outside her back door smoking a cigarette. She is lit from above.

The two white men who share the flat above hers are in their kitchen. The fleshier man with the hipster beard is washing up, his younger-looking partner moving easily around him. Above them, the kitchen of the top flat is in darkness. The youngish dark-haired woman who lives there, possibly alone, is seen more often in the daytime, staring into the middle distance waiting for the kettle to boil.

The woman in the red dress is still smoking. She looks up. Nick steps back even though there's no possibility of her being able to see him in the shadows. He has switched off the under-cupboard lighting and there is no incoming light that might catch the lenses of his binoculars.

The Asian couple top left are in their kitchen. Her at the sink, him hovering. White vest. Blur as binoculars sweep across flats and stop on Spartan kitchen top right lit by single strip light, owner absent. Two flats below, the empty flat, empty for weeks. Ground floor, bottom right. Bathroom light, though, now. Slowly moving pale shape behind frosted glass. Someday someone will invent a lens, a filter, an app, to unencrypt frosted glass. Find the right focal length, move in, back off, pixelated images becoming coherent. Bathroom light goes out. Light leaks into kitchen. Well-built woman appears, hair wrapped in a towel.

In the mornings the sun shines directly into the flats opposite. Nick stands at the sink. The woman on the ground floor is washing the pots. The woman two storeys above is staring into space. Then she lifts a kettle into and out of the frame. The man in the white vest is standing, alone, in his kitchen.

To the right, the newcomer, the well-built woman, is in her kitchen on the ground floor, moving around, opening and closing doors. She exits stage right, reappears outside, by the door to her store cupboard. She twists the handle, pulls on it, tugs. Bends down, picks up a small hammer. She bangs away at something on the frame of the door. Stands back, hands on hips. Takes a red hanky from the pocket of her jogging pants, wipes her face. Lifts and agitates the front of her top for ventilation.

Nick puts down the binoculars and moves away from the sink. He opens the fridge and takes out a beer. From the top drawer he takes the bottle opener, from the cupboard a glass. He pours the beer and moves back to the sink. He puts the empty glass on the draining board and turns to the drawers, opening the third one down and taking out the claw hammer. He takes his keys and leaves the flat. The sun beats down upon his head as he walks across the courtyard. The well-built woman is still trying to remove something – a bent nail perhaps – from the door frame. She stops when he approaches, turns round.

'Hi,' says Nick. 'My name's Neil.'

Nick returns home with a bag of shopping and walks up the stairs. He stops on the first-floor landing. On the wall outside the flat of his downstairs neighbour a framed picture has appeared. He stands and looks at it. While he is looking, a door opens above. Given that there are only two flats on each floor, and this is a day for Freya to be at her mum's, it must be his landing neighbour, James. He listens to James's footsteps and waits for him to be almost upon him before turning away from the picture.

'Oh, hi, James,' says Nick.

'Hi, Neil,' says James.

Nick doesn't move for a moment. Then, with James already halfway down the next flight, Nick leans over the bannister, saying, 'Nick,' in a slightly choked voice.

James makes a noise – half grunt, half laugh – of acknowledgement and looks up, without stopping. Within seconds he has turned the corner and is on the ground floor. Nick continues to climb and while he stands outside his own flat trying to find the right key he turns and looks at the empty wall adjacent to his flat.

Once inside, he dumps his shopping, then turns to the kitchen drawers. He slides open the third drawer down and takes out a claw hammer and a jar of nails. In his bedroom three framed pictures lean against the wall. He picks one and returns to the landing. The nail goes in easily and he hangs the picture and steps back to check that it's straight.

Insufficient Data for an Image

It was last thing at night, the first time I noticed it. I was lying in bed, looking at the crossword, both bedside lamps on even though Patricia's side of the bed was empty. She always re-marked on my preference for things in pairs. Both bedside lamps had to be on – or off – at the same time. Both our towels side by side on the towel rail in the bathroom – or both in the wash. It was a matter of balance, I told her.

I was struggling with that week's crossword and it didn't help that there was a fly blundering around in my peripheral vision. I flapped my hand half-heartedly before I remembered it was the middle of winter and there were no flies. I was tired, my vision was failing through exhaustion, I told myself. I put the crossword down and switched off the light. Then I reached across and switched off Patricia's light, too.

In the morning, not only was my vision normal, but I had forgotten the disturbance of the night before. I still struggled with the crossword. If I'm honest, I'd been struggling with it for weeks. I couldn't remember the last time I'd finished one and sent it off.

That night, or the next night, it happened again. This time it was less like a fly and more like how I imagined – or tried to remember – it might feel to have an unruly lock of hair dangling at the edge of your vision.

Patricia had experienced a similar phenomenon, although during the hours of daylight, and I had encouraged her to go and see Ragini, who I had been going to for years, and get checked out. Floaters, Ragini had told her. Tiny pieces of debris caught in the vitreous humour. (Like inclusions in amber, I suggested.) They could flutter like flakes of ash or suddenly intrude like a twig on a low branch. After a while, Ragini said, you stop noticing them. And she did.

I didn't stop noticing mine, but I had work to do. I had a deadline. To be more accurate, my colleague Sarah and I had a deadline. It was the first time we had collaborated and at this rate it would be the last. Sarah had been to the library, or searched the online catalogue, and sent me the results of her search. I opened one of the PDFs. She listed book after book after book. None of them sounded as if it was likely to yield anything. But the problem wasn't the books, or Sarah. The problem was me. I had lost count of the number of times I had emailed Sarah to apologise for failing to send anything. She had said if it was a bad time we could just pull out of the project. We didn't really know each other, were not even in the same department, but had been paired by the organiser of the project.

Then I saw there was actually a problem with the PDF. The text relating to book 13 on the list would not load on screen. Instead there was a pop-up that read: *Insufficient data for an image.*

Like Junction 13 on the M56, I said to Sarah in an email via the work server.

Or the thirteenth floor of an American skyscraper, Sarah replied, except there was a different reason for that. More accurately, there was a different reason for Junction 13 on the M56, I wrote back. The thirteenth floor of an American skyscraper was *there*, it *existed*, it was *present*, but it was renamed the four-teenth floor, for reasons of superstition. Whereas Junction 13 of the M56 simply wasn't there.

Sarah wondered if it *was* there, but for some reason I couldn't see it.

I said that was an interesting idea, before quitting out of the work email.

I sat at my desk and tried to work on the piece. There was a fault with my laptop. The black border around the screen seemed to be leaking on to the left-hand side of the desktop. I peered closer and the black edging grew larger. At the same time I noticed a faint mark, like the shadow of a spent match, on the right of the screen. I closed the laptop and saw that the black column and the spent match were now projected on to the pile of papers between the laptop and the wall. I got up from the desk and went to the window. It was harder to make out the black shapes against the bare branches of the trees.

I drew the curtains and lay on the bed. Some years earlier I had experienced painless migraines marked by visual distur-bances. People spoke of flashing lights, but mine glowed like the filament of a lightbulb. The only way to make them go away was to lie down in a darkened room. I got under the duvet and stretched my arm across to Patricia's side of the bed, which was cool. I turned over on to my right side and moved across into her space, clasping my arms around my knees and pulling them up against my chest. I pressed my face into her pillow and imagined I could smell her.

Later, I sat at the kitchen table and opened the laptop. The black shapes had disappeared. My personal inbox was full of emails from people saying nice things about Patricia. I opened them and closed them like so many doors. I got up from the table and opened the fridge. There wasn't much in there, but it didn't smell very good, so I closed it again and closed my laptop. I went around the flat closing anything that was open. Windows – always a couple left open even in the winter – and doors and boxes and drawers that had been left open just a little bit or that wouldn't close until I made them close. I got into bed with my clothes on and switched off my light and then Patricia's light and pulled the duvet over my head.

I woke in the early hours aware that I had dreamt about Patricia, but unable to remember even a single frame. My head was throbbing. I went to the bathroom and took some pills and got back into bed.

I didn't wake again until morning. Everything looked normal. I went to the fridge to get milk for tea, but then remembered and made green tea instead. I opened my laptop, determined to finish the piece for the collaboration, but when I looked at the screen, I couldn't see it for an irregular latticework of shadowy grey-black lines and geometric shapes. I stared at them, trying to see through them or past them, trying to work out if they were something new that had been inserted and now existed between me and the world or if they were   nothing gaps   holes   in my perception of reality. Had something been added or had something been taken away?

I dimly remembered the titles sequence of a film I had seen as a young man. A long shot, possibly a road, I couldn't remember. A thin black alien shape appeared on the screen. It didn't make any sense. Then another, a different shape, just as meaningless. Strange, cut-out shapes. Shards. Slowly you realised this was type, or the black background out of which type would be reversed. Gradually it acquired meaning, imprisoning the images as it did so, communicating an overpowering sense of doom.

I went to lie down, but couldn't get back to sleep. In the

bathroom I looked at my face in the mirror. It had been cut up and reassembled. I looked at the two toothbrushes in the mug. Patricia's was dry; I used mine.

I put on several layers of clothing because I imagined I would have to walk slowly. I called ahead while en route. Ragini agreed to see me. I pushed open the door. A look of almost loving concern on her face. She asked how I was. She put her hand on my arm and said, How long has it been?

Since my last test?

She frowned.

I explained what was happening. I've always wondered, I told her, what it must be like to live in one of those houses – those new houses – where they've stuck diamond leading on all the windows.

Ragini led me upstairs and closed the shutters. I sat in the chair and she leant over me, minty breath in my face, the soft pressure of her thigh against my leg. In the darkness, I felt something close to happiness. Look into my light, she whispered. Look into my light.

Someone Take These Dreams Away

When *Control* opened at the Cornerhouse, the nights were getting longer. Most days, it was dark by half past four. Anton Corbijn's biopic of Ian Curtis was the film of the year; everybody went to see it (apart from me), even Nick. But while the rest of our colleagues from English & Film would have allowed themselves to become immersed in Corbijn's recreation of late 70s Manchester, marvelling at Martin Ruhe's black and white cinematography, Nick would have been sitting there in the dark thinking of another British film with only a handful of scenes shot in black and white, the rest in colour.

Nick has a thing about black and white. He's fond of quoting Christopher Walken's line from Donald Cammell's *Wild Side*. 'Life is black and white. Have you ever seen grey squares on a chessboard?'

I'm sitting in front of his computer in the office we've shared since I recommended him for a vacant lecturer's post, and I'm wondering where to look first. I don't even know how much stuff he keeps on his desktop machine. I hardly use mine at all, preferring my laptop.

The office is tiny – the university has a problem with overcrowding – but it's surprising how sitting at Nick's desk gives me an entirely different perspective on it. The difference between it and the view from my desk is like the difference between the way *to* somewhere and the journey *back*. I spin slowly round to look at Nick's shelves. Two books by Roy Armes, *A Critical History of British Cinema* and *The Ambiguous Image*. Roger Manvell's *New Cinema in Britain*. Danny Peary's *Cult Movies*. (I have a copy of that somewhere, too.) A few annual-sized hardbacks – *Thriller Movies, A Pictorial History of Crime Films, Photoplay Film Yearbook 1976*. I was struck by how many of these titles dated back to the 1970s. Among the newer stuff: Chris Darke's *Light Readings*, Ali Catterall and Simon Wells's book about British cult films *Your Face Here*, and a recent edition of the *Time Out Film Guide*. An eclectic library.

It's very quiet in the office, which it rarely was when Nick was around. He'd either be banging away at his keyboard ('Touch-typing's for puffs. No offence') or complaining loudly into his phone about the standard of the technical equipment in the lecture theatres. Or he'd have a student in for a tutorial. Three people in an office designed for one. Admin, teaching, dealing with students – that's only half of what we're supposed to be doing. The rest – our so-called research – is what brings in the real money. But if we want a quiet space in which to write, there's no point looking anywhere near the university.

18.8.87 [morning]

In a TV studio where I've been interviewed. The Queen turns up. Then we all go out to a tube station. The Queen looks nervous. On the train a man is smoking a cigarette and a cigar. His fat cigar looks like a penis. Arriving at Cambridge University (!?) I am shown with one other person (?) to my room, which is room B at school. I am given keys, though the door is of the saloon bar type.

On the upper shelves behind Nick's desk, the beautifully tactile, plastic-sheathed cases of DVDs. *Elephant*, *Old Boy*, *If....*, *Zéro de conduite.* Beautiful things, DVDs. Simple, full of promise. How many have you bought and never watched? In case you ever needed to see something again, to write about it, you told yourself, but really it was just to possess them. Like a director hoarding prints of his own films. A sense of ownership, a piece of marketing genius. At least half the DVDs in anyone's collection have never been watched.

I notice the line from *Wild Side* written on a yellow Post-it stuck to the side of Nick's inkjet printer. Also, on another Post-it alongside: 'When do we live? That's what I want to know.' I knew the quote. It was a line spoken by Mick Travis, the Malcolm McDowell character in *If....*, near the beginning of the film. I might not have known it had it not been for Nick's interest in the film. His obsession with the film.

I've been covering for him for a week now. Delivering a lecture to undergraduates, running a workshop with his MA students. His absence has been noticed, but has not yet become a serious problem. It will, though. The conference he's organised – *Run in the Corridor: the Politics of School Shootings on Film*, which he's been working towards for several months – is only a week away.

A couple of times in the last few days I've been convinced things have switched around on his desk and have wondered if he's been in during the night. I know he has a good relationship with Byron, the dreadlocked security guard who wanders in from Moss Side towards the end of the afternoon. I've seen the two of them sharing a roll-up, huddled against the autumnal chill and standing a cautious distance from the main entrance to the building. One of them sources the gear and supplies the other. My guess is Byron is the supplier, if only because Nick, for all his strengths, is not very streetwise. But he can turn on the charm. One afternoon while he was waiting for a female student to turn up for a tutorial, he told me she was dyslexic. Listen to this, he said, reading from the student's Learning Support Document: "'Linzi has difficulty with planning work, prioritising tasks and concentrating when there is background noise. She has poor short-term memory and may lose flow when interrupted.'" He looked up at me. 'For fuck's sake,' he said. 'Do you think *I'm* dyslexic, then?'

'Sounds like we all are,' I said.

When Linzi came in and sat down across the desk from Nick, he held up a print-out and said to her, 'This is your Learning Support Document.' He immediately crumpled it into a ball and threw it at the bin. When she looked shocked, he said, 'It's bollocks. I don't care how you spell encyclopaedia – consensus – liaison. Whatever. I'm interested in the *content* of what you write, not its *appearance*.' She looked uncertain. 'Don't worry,' he said with a resigned smile. 'I can always print off another copy.'

In the quiet of the early afternoon, the phone rings on Nick's desk. I look at it, wondering whether to pick it up. I don't look at it for very long.

'Hello? Nick's phone,' I say, strongly hoping the caller will not respond by saying, 'Hello, Nick's phone.'

'I'm looking for Nick,' says a female voice.

You and me both.

'He's not at his desk at the moment, I'm afraid,' I say. 'Would you like to leave a message?'

'That's OK,' she says, and before I know it she is gone.

I dial 1471.

We are sorry. We do not have the caller's number.

I remember my own student days. One of my lecturers,

Roger Huss – one of the few I really liked – had invited me to call him by his first name, and maybe I did a couple of times, but it never felt right somehow. *Excuse me, Roger. Thank you, Roger.* Now it's different. It's *Hey Nick* and *Laters dude.* Student reps sit on staff committees and complain bitterly if they think they're not getting their money's worth.

7.1.96

At school, a gang of lads gathers round. I bristle but say nothing. Another lad comes in and tells us what we have to do – look back over all the films of the year and see which one God would have made differently (!).

In my mind, as I hang up the phone, is a picture of Helena Swan, one of Nick's postgraduate students, a well-built and un-deniably attractive woman in her early fifties. I've noticed her hanging around at the end of Nick's seminars, laughing at his jokes during a staff-students social event. I've had to start leaving the room when she comes for tutorials with Nick. It was her voice on the phone, I'm sure of it.

I switch his computer on. I know Nick's log-in because he dictated it to me over the phone one day when a system error was blocking mine and I couldn't use the photocopier. I enter it and the prompt asks for a password. I have a few weak guesses – anderson, mcdowell, elephant (if.... doesn't have enough characters) – but don't get lucky.

I stand up and go over to the window. Looking out at the windswept junction of side roads, I am reminded for some reason of another time I stood in exactly the same position and looked out to see Nick sauntering towards the building and talking on his mobile. He had been smiling. I didn't often see him smile. As he approached the barrier, which was lowered to keep out unauthorised vehicles, he ended the call and dropped the phone into his jeans pocket. In front of him, the barrier suddenly rose as if, grandly, permitting him to enter. Nick looked up and gave a great guffawing laugh, which was even rarer than a smile and made him look a lot younger than his forty-five years. I could hear it, two floors up and through double-glazing. I laughed as well and felt momentarily light-headed as well as lighthearted. It felt like the first time we'd really connected in years, perhaps since school, though of course he hadn't seen me watching, and by the time he'd reached our office, his face had settled into its semi-permanent grimace of disapproval.

I go to the department admin office on the third floor. On the left as you go in is a series of filing cabinets. I open the one labelled S-Z and flick through until I find what I want. I leaf through a file, make some notes, and leave.

I stop by our office to pick up my bag and am about to leave when I have a thought. I walk over to Nick's shelves and take down the DVD of *If....* and a couple of books and slip them into my bag.

22.1.96 [morning]
Attending hospital. Very soon it's become our old school – it's assembly time. We're all in uniform. There's a boy in a wheelchair near me. He's got a glass of Coca-Cola with ice. Another boy comes along and sits in another wheelchair, sliding a big brown suitcase underneath the chair. I know the suitcase contains weapons.

The bus is full of students. I stare out of the window and find myself thinking about Iain Constable's recent lecture on research methods. He was coming across as rather pedantic with his insistence on correct presentation. Footnotes, quotations, bibliographies. Everything had to be just so, or the student would lose marks. 'Right down to the number of dots in an ellipsis,' he said, and Nick spoke up, saying, 'What about *If….*? What if you need to mention the title of Lindsay Anderson's 1968 film *If….*, which famously has four dots in its ellipsis? What then?' Iain laughed and Nick said he wasn't joking, it was a serious point. Taking Nick's interruption as a challenge, Iain entrenched and said an ellipsis with four dots was a mistake and would be marked as such in any work he came across. 'Good job I'm not your student, then,' Nick said, as he got up and walked out of the lecture theatre.

I found him later in our office, in tears.

'What is it?' I asked, shocked.

'Nothing. Leave me alone,' he snapped, then softened slightly. 'Just give us a minute, Mike.'

I went to see the head of department about a timetabling issue. When I came back, Nick had dried his eyes, but his face was red as it jutted towards his computer screen.

'Are you going to tell me what's wrong or shall I mind my own business?' I asked.

'Something I read in here,' Nick said, picking up Ali Catterall and Simon Wells's *Your Face Here*, which I knew had a chapter on *If….* He opened the book and flicked through the pages. 'Page 64,' he said and chucked the book across the office.

I caught it and turned to the right page.

'Last par,' Nick said. '"There were plans for a school re-union".'

Writing about Anderson's idea for a proper sequel to *If….* (as distinct from the fluff that was *O Lucky Man!*), the authors caught the reader up on what had happened to key cast members. Christine Noonan (the Girl) had left the profession and gone into teaching, David Wood had become a children's writer and McDowell, of course, had moved to Hollywood. Two, however, were dead. Richard Warwick (Wallace) had died from an AIDS-related condition in 1997, and Rupert Webster (Bobby Phillips) had been knifed to death on the New York subway in the 1980s.

I felt a lump in my throat as I instantly recalled one of their scenes from the film, shot in black and white, in which they slept side by side in Wallace's bed. Although Malcolm McDowell's scene with the Girl at the Packhorse Cafe, in which they had ended up play-fighting naked on the floor, again in black and white, had been remarkably effective in its insistence that fantasy was very much a part of the film's reality, it was clear where the director believed the emotional heart of the film was to be found. The camera's slow glide across the dorm, showing first Bobby Phillips and then revealing Wallace lying next to him, had made that very clear. Earlier, Phillips had watched admiringly as Wallace, after flashing a smile at the younger boy, performed slow-motion acrobatics on the high bar.

Although the scene in the Packhorse Cafe was sexually explicit, even allowing a glimpse of pubic hair, the film's erotic peak was to be found later, Nick had once patiently explained to me, in another black and white sequence. The one in which the blonde Mrs Kemp, housemaster Arthur Lowe's wife, played by Mary McLeod, walks naked down an empty corridor towards the camera, and then, away from the camera, through a boys' dormitory, trailing a hand along a line of washbasins and turning, finally, to look back over her shoulder at the viewer, her stance recalling that of the Girl in the cafe as she looked round from under a curtain of thick, dark hair while making coffee for Mick and Johnny. Mrs Kemp looked over her right shoulder, the Girl over her left. One of these shots looked as if it was meant to be erotic, but was merely a tease, a stock pose, a nod to the classic black-and-whites; the other, exploiting the full-figured vulnerability of the childless and lonely Mrs Kemp, actually was and powerfully so.

'If only Mary McLeod knew how many adolescent boys' fantasies she was responsible for,' Nick said.

This comment comes back to me as I get off the bus in West Didsbury. The anonymous Edwardian conversion across the road, once home to Factory Records, reveals no trace of its cultural significance. I cross Lapwing Lane and keep walking. The address I'm looking for is located within a grid of quiet residential streets to the west of Palatine Road. Helena Swan is not quite another generation, as Mrs Kemp had been to Mick, Johnny and the other boys ('Do you need this, Mrs Kemp,' Mick had asked, in one of the refectory scenes, with a provocative thrust of the sauce bottle), but she is an apparently available woman some ten years older than Nick, of a similar build to Mary McLeod in 1968. She could easily be a stand-in, a body double.

A narrow footpath runs down the side of Helena Swan's property. Barely wide enough for two people to squeeze past each other, it offers a convenient spot from which to observe the back of the house. Some lights are burning; no noise can be heard. There must be a better way to go about what I'm trying to achieve. Do I really expect to see Nick suddenly appear silhouetted in a bedroom window? To knock on the front door and explain my quest would embroider unnecessary complications on to an already elaborate tapestry. I decide to wait for a while.

Wednesday 15 January 1997
At a swimming baths, there are three pools but they're short and narrow, barely bigger than normal bathroom baths. The one in the middle has two

people in it: someone on the left who remains still, and a young black man who is swimming lengths. There would just be room for me to swim to his right. I'm perched on the rim about to dive in but I worry that my arms or legs might disturb other diners because now it's a restaurant as well. Also the young man has just smiled at me and he's naked and I'm worried there isn't enough room.

My thoughts turn to the DVD in my bag. Assuming a lack of success in my current endeavour, I will play the film when I get home. I've seen it a number of times and my familiarity with it has been enhanced by Nick's frequent allusions and references, but to watch it again under these particular conditions might just throw up an idea or two. I could never forget the grey echoing corridors down which Mick, Johnny and Wallace confidently stride, three abreast, to meet their punishment at the hands of the Whips. Vicious lashes of the cane in the school gymnasium, the wooden floor pounding with the lengthy run-up of the sadistic Rowntree. How similar that gym was to our own, in the grammar school. How different were the relationships of abuse, yet how familiar, really.

I take out my notebook, then my mobile, and key in a number. I hear a faint ringing, then another light comes on in the kitchen window and Helena Swan appears. She picks up the phone.

'Hello?' she says. 'Hello?'

I hold my breath.

'Who is this?'

Still I say nothing.

Then, her voice shrinking to a whisper: '*Nick?*'

I thumb the red button to break the connection and breathe out and quickly breathe in again. I watch as Helena Swan turns away from the phone and stares into the air in front of her face, which looks as if it has just been slapped. I wish at that point I hadn't done what I have done, in spite of the information gained from it.

I asked Nick once if he was frustrated by the confusion surrounding the use of black and white sequences in *If….*, for the most part a colour film. Every commentator seems to have a different take and all claim to be reflecting the position of director Lindsay Anderson. Some say it was done to save money, others that a consistency of colour tone in the chapel, with its great stained-glass windows, could not be achieved. Still others argue that the choice was aesthetic, that it had to do with reminding the viewer of Anderson's links to Free Cinema, that it was part of a general push for Brechtian alienation, that it was intended to heighten the tension between fantasy and reality.

'It's all of those things and none of them,' he'd said. 'Art's impossible without ambiguity.'

4 May 1997

Standing at a urinal in our school, but in Scotland. A man stood too close to me so I moved along and he muttered that the only person I'd have something to worry about in that department would be Ian somebody. I challenged him. He shook water at me, which I soon realised was his piss. I grabbed him and demanded to know his name and where he worked – Iain Grant, lab technician, he said. Somehow I knew they were two different Ians and that this one spelled his name the Scottish way.

When I get back home, I pour myself a large glass of wine and watch the film again. Every shot of the school reminds me of the one Nick and I both attended, he five years ahead of me. A couple of years ago there was a reunion. It was the last opportunity to visit the school, as the governors had finally admitted defeat in a long battle against time and announced that the school would move to new premises at the beginning of the next academic year. I asked Nick if he was going.

'Am I fuck.'

I went; I was curious. You were supposed to get a boy to show you around, but I slipped up the back stairs and prowled the upper corridors on my own. I wasn't hugely keen to catch up with old faces and was attracted more by the fabric of the building itself. There were textures and shapes I had forgotten, but which came back to me with startling clarity once I saw them again after two decades. The painted noticeboards pierced by thousands of pin holes. The grey plastic roller doors on boys' lockers outside classrooms.

The swimming pool was unrecognisable. Gone were the cold, green tiles, the constant drip of freezing water from the concertina glass ceiling. The pool had always been my most hated part of the school, even after optional wearing of trunks was introduced half-way through my time there. Until I was fourteen or fifteen, all boys swam naked, and all boys found it humiliating and degrading. Mature adolescents, late developers – I was never sure which subset found it more embarrassing.

In the refectory I saw Corky – Mr McCorkindale, games master – and felt a sudden jolt of discomfort. I hovered on the edge of a group of old boys to overhear the conversation between them and Corky, who looked older (obviously), but also considerably smaller, than I remembered him. I already knew that he had left teaching, and I heard him say he had retrained as a psychotherapist. One of the old boys burst out laughing. Corky laughed, too, but then asked what was funny.

'Well, you created your own client base, didn't you?' said the former pupil. 'With the school's policy on swimwear.'

We could see the funny side now, but it had been nothing to laugh about at the time. Some had got over it; others were left with intimacy issues. I know one old boy turned Sunday league footballer who has never felt comfortable showering with his team-mates after a game. *I just can't get naked in front of other men*, he told me, paraphrasing Woody Allen. Not a problem I've ever had.

Nick never asked me about the reunion and I didn't volunteer anything. Part of me wanted to tell him that I had tried the door at the back of the school theatre, but that it had been locked.

Rewatching *If….* reminds me of the importance of Bobby Phillips. Not only do he and Wallace share a bed, but the younger boy finds himself up on the roof with Mick, Johnny, Wallace and the Girl at the end of the film, bristling with guns and ammunition. A loaded gun won't set you free? Depends who you're pointing it at.

Sunday 31 October 1999
[Halloween.] I was back at school. The corridors and great hall were familiar, but everywhere there were orange plastic girders and supports appearing to hold up the ceilings. I knew these would be unsuitable to bear any loads, yet they could have no other use that I could fathom.

The film has given me no clearer idea how to find Nick. From my bag I take out the books I borrowed from his shelves – a short BFI monograph on the film and his copy of *Your Face Here*, which falls open at page 64 and the paragraph about Rupert Webster and Richard Warwick. I have a look at the chapter on *If….* and then the BFI book, by Mark Sinker, which is intelligently written and packed with ideas and different approaches to interpretation. I notice that *Your Face Here* records the location of the motorcycle showroom, from which Mick and Johnny steal the motorbike they drive to the Packhorse

Cafe, as being in South Wimbledon, whereas the BFI book and other sources, both print and internet, maintain it's in Shepherd's Bush. I look up *Your Face Here* on Amazon and am interested to see it has nine five-star reader reviews, all posted by 'A Customer'. None of them goes into much detail. On a hunch, I google Richard Warwick: died at the age of 52 with a form of dementia brought on by AIDS. For Rupert Webster, however, I find a couple of sources claiming he's still alive. Either Anderson or McDowell spread a rumour that he'd been killed, they said. The internet is notoriously unreliable and it's only sentimentality that makes me place more trust in the printed page. I don't know what to believe, but I do hope that the boys who wrote *Your Face Here*, a lively and enjoyable read, are wrong and that Rupert Webster, who for a short time forty years ago was Bobby Phillips, is alive.

More to the point, I hope Nick is alive.

I'm narrowing down my options. I realise I have to do something I should have done days ago.

I grab my stuff and leave the house.

The building containing Nick's flat is only a couple of streets away from Helena Swan's house. I'm wondering if she knows this, as I tell a resident on the top floor that I'm delivering pizzas. The door clicks open while he's still asking his girlfriend if they've ordered any.

Sunday 27 November 2005
Looking through old copies of the school newspaper, I see one with a picture of a girl on the front page. I recognise her, but the name given − something Schneidor − is not familiar. There are pictures of me, black and white, milking the applause from a huge crowd. There are other pictures of crowds on the fields at the front of the school, among them a young Mike, looking at me and waving. He moves as the picture comes to life.

I've never been to Nick's place – he's never invited me – but I know he lives on the first floor. There are two doors on the first landing. The one on the right has pounding music coming from within, so I knock once on the door on the left, wait a moment, then lean my shoulder against it. I feel it give very slightly, so I treat it to a shove, then another, and I'm inside. I push the door to behind me and lean against it as I wait for my heartbeat to return to normal.

Straight ahead is a tiny bathroom. To the left of that an equally small bedroom. Facing the bedroom is a combined kitchen and living room. Given the size of the flat, a professional would be able to toss it in two minutes and leave with either what they came for or the knowledge that it wasn't there to be found. I'm not a professional, but I do know Nick. I check out the bookshelves. More film books. Novels about cinema: *Flicker*, *Throat Sprockets*, *The House of Sleep*. An edition of *Halliwell's Film Guide*. I take it down and look up *If....*, which Halliwell appears to admire but still attacks for its 'fashionable emphasis on obscure narrative', concluding that 'the film as a whole makes no discernible point'. Halliwell just couldn't help himself.

On the next shelf down are copies of Nick's books. His studies of Westerns and Eastern European SF and fantasy cinema for Wallflower Press and the experimental novel that was published in a limited edition by a local independent outfit. There are not many of us who have read it.

There's a decent-sized plasma-screen TV, but nothing leaps out at me from Nick's collection of DVDs and tapes, and there's no sign of a laptop (and no room for a desktop). The bedroom is dominated by an unmade double bed, on the far side of which a fat, well-thumbed notebook sits on a little set of drawers. It appears to be a dream diary. I flick through it and read random entries.

In school, towards the end of the day, I find myself near an empty staircase leading up, so I go up, thinking I'll just have a look around. I end up in a maths classroom full of small boys. The uniform is different and there are variations. I see one boy in a tight-fitting blazer and trousers that's very dark grey with silver symbols in a regular pattern all over it. The boys are getting up to go. I want to leave before them. I pass the teacher who has grey hair and who I think I recognise from my time at the school. He has his back to me. Then I'm looking for the door and I can't find it. Finally I do, but it's hidden and to get through it you have to push drapes aside and step over a threshold of broken bits of wood – it feels like a trap.

They're not *all* about school, but enough of them are.

I put the notebook back down. On an impulse I open the top drawer and immediately wish I hadn't.

I was going to hail a cab, but when I get back to Palatine Road there's a bus coming, so I stick my hand out. I imagine everyone on the bus can see the way my jacket is weighed down on one side, but I doubt I'm the first person to catch the 43 bus with a loaded gun in his pocket. I wonder how he got hold of it, though when I think about it, there must be a hundred ways to get tooled up in Manchester these days.

I get off a couple of stops early and walk. I haven't been back since the reunion. The fence by the old biology block never was much of a barrier. I approach the main buildings from the side. Much less conspicuous than using the front entrance. I don't know what plans exist for the disused school. Demolition and a highly lucrative land sale, I presume. For now it stands empty. I enter via the ramp down to the basement on the west side. One of the double doors at the bottom opens at my touch. If the signs posted by a security company are anything other than an empty threat, I'd be surprised. I pick my way past a line of toilets, not a single door remaining, broken glass on the concrete floor flashing in the weak light of my mobile phone. I climb the stairs to the corner of the maths and geography corridors, where I stop and listen. All I can hear is the thumping of my heart and a steady drip-drip-drip somewhere behind me.

I creep past the Great Hall and main stairs. The shadows are grainy, alive with glittering motes. I hesitate outside the Masters' Common Room, the smooth stones of the corridor floor carpeted with white dust and flakes of paint. In the theatre, the individual wooden blocks that make up the parquet floor are all loose. The door at the back is no longer locked, but Nick is not inside. I enter a room I have not been inside for almost thirty years, at least not outside my dreams. Night after night, sometimes, for several days at a time, I have found myself back here. Twice, at the most, we were here together, but in my mind the narratives of those two occasions have become intertwined with the many, many times I have dreamed myself back. If the closest I can get to Nick in reality is sharing duties and an office, in my fantasy life we have remained locked into an infinite variety of positions on two turquoise vinyl-covered chairs pushed together as a makeshift couch in this tiny room – props cupboard? Wardrobe department? – at the back of the theatre. The first time, early May 1980, he had a little Philips cassette player and a badly recorded tape of bass-heavy music, dark and threatening, but utterly compelling. I asked him what it was and he smiled as he said it was called *Unknown Pleasures*. Even with the unsophisticated musical tastes of a twelve-year-old, I could tell it was special. The way the drummer played just off the beat, the fact that the bass player carried the melody more often than not. Nick described the singer to me, told me he suffered epileptic fits, sometimes during performances.

99

When he touched me, it felt both wrong and right at the same time, but he was tender and patient. I liked his smile and the smell of his neck. When he held my face with his hands and kissed me, I imagined the east and west wings of the main school building somehow wrapping themselves around this tiny room at the back of the theatre and keeping us safe.

The second time, just before the Whit week holiday, Nick told me that the singer from the band had killed himself. He played the album again and we sat in the dark listening to it, the lyrics scattered with clues that should have foretold the singer's suicide. Nick also told me about a film he had seen on television just over a year ago in which four schoolboys and a girl staged a bloody revolution at their boarding school, shooting the headmaster and killing dozens of pupils and teachers. *We're in that film*, he told me. *You and me. One day you'll see it and you'll see what I mean.*

As I reach out an arm to steady myself against the wall, I feel the weight of the gun in my pocket.

I re-enter the auditorium and head for the swing doors that lead back to the main corridor. The eroded hollows in the steps cushion my footfalls as I climb the main stairs. The upper corridors are lit by moonlight. I stop and look out across the quad towards the windows of the adjacent corridor where a moving figure catches my eye. The pale, wide-hipped body, silvery white hair. Black holes for eyes. I don't need to be any closer to know that Helena Swan is playing Mrs Kemp, which would place Nick most likely at the end of her corridor at the junction with mine. I keep walking, the weight of the gun tugging at my right shoulder.

When I reach the junction of the two corridors, Nick is not there. I figure he'll be half way up the next one, so that in a moment he can have Helena Swan walk away from him and look back, just as Mrs Kemp does. I doubt he's gone to the trouble of bringing a camera, but am aware that if I approach now I will ruin his shot. So be it.

He steps out from behind a bank of lockers twenty yards away.

'I wondered when you'd come,' he says.

Helena Swan falters and stands still, uncertain how to react.

'You shouldn't be walking around with that in your pocket,' Nick says calmly. 'Give it to me.'

I take the gun out of my pocket. Helena Swan, on seeing the dark shape in my hand, turns and runs towards the far end of the corridor.

'Who is it for?' I ask.

Nick smiles. 'You brought it,' he points out.

'I couldn't leave it in your flat with the door off its hinges,' I say. 'But if I give it to you, I'm worried you just might use it. Whether here and now or next week at your conference, in a dramatic re-enactment of a certain film.'

'"One man can change the world with a bullet in the right place",' he says, quoting Mick Travis. 'I'm not sure I can face that conference. All those academics.'

I remain silent, thinking. He has a secret he can't live with. I am it.

'So,' he says.

Maths Tower

The Maths Tower was built in 1969. Two hundred and forty-six feet high. Seventy-five metres. Thirty-six years later, a girl called Nina is sitting in Manchester Museum, across the road from the Maths Tower, watching at the window. Nina's parents enrolled as students in 1984. They met in the Maths Tower. One plus one equals two. Eight months later, in 1985, they scored over 90 per cent in their first-year exams and celebrated in a quiet corner on the fifth floor. Nine months on, four days early, Nina was born. She hadn't been planned and the strain broke them apart. Nina's father simply deducted himself from the equation and Nina's mother found it hard to cope. The sums didn't add up. Eighty pounds for a gram. Ten quid for twenty minutes. Two months in Styal prison. Nina went through eight foster homes in half as many years. When she started school she could barely count to three.

Fifteen years later, aged nineteen, she's a daily visitor to the museum, parting the curtains in the Ancient Egyptian room. She spends twice as long with these mummies as she did with her own. But her attention is fixed on the activity across the street. The scaffolding went up in the spring and plastic sheeting followed it, stretched like skin around the outside of the

103

steel poles. Two hundred and six bones make up the human skeleton. If you jumped from the top of the Maths Tower you'd break at least half of them. When the tower is completely sheathed, the magic trick is ready. Slowly the covering is peeled back, from the top down, day by day, to reveal that the tower within has vanished. The trick takes a couple of weeks. Nina watches every day as a fine haze envelops the sheathed structure. Then the remaining plastic is removed in one go and the scaffold seems to tighten its joints and dig into the stump of the tower, an exoskeleton turning on its freight. The hard hats swarm, the orange vehicles growl and churn through the mud. The ever-shortening tower mutates. A caricature of a Balkan house, upper storeys overhanging. An air traffic controllers' observation deck. An East Berlin watchtower. When a yellow articulated arm reaches up dinosaur-like to close pincer jaws on concrete, a redundant tuft of steel cable springs forth like a sheared fan of muscle fibres – and with it billows a small cloud of tiny numbers.

Each new bite the mechanical jaws take out of the building releases another puff of digits, floating like seeds on the wind. It seems they are what held the tower together and now they are out in the world. A 2 lands on the front of a passing bus, which slows down and takes the next turning, following a new route. The wind blows a 4 on to the blue shirt of a football fan walking by, changing the identity of his favourite player. A geography student gives her mobile number to a boy she met the night before, but when he texts her later the message will be received by a female paramedic attending an emergency call.

Nina studies the ground at the foot of the tower. Each workman's boot that strikes the earth detonates a tiny explosion of numbers. Long strings of figures smoke out of the mountains of rubble and twist into the air where they cross the sky like banners pulled by invisible planes. Misconnections abound across the city as phone numbers on adverts and signs are replaced by those for petrochemical companies in Abu Dhabi and exclusive escort agencies operating Cheshire-wide out of Prestbury.

Numerical chaos reigns throughout the autumn. The remains of the tower are gradually razed and by December the diggers are crisscrossing level ground, over and over, round and round, trampling the remaining digits into the dirt. Nina lifts her eyes and stares through the faint haze where the tower once stood, until it finally dissipates in the cold, bright sunshine and all she can see are the snow-capped hills of the Peaks in the distance.

Nothing Else Matters

Take your glasses off to wipe your eyes and everything in the distance loses definition. What is that down there? Right at the end. A snooker table? It looks a lot like one. Bright lights suspended over green baize, clink of ball against ball. Oh look, that could be me, sitting close to the table, wearing an old jacket that's two sizes too big and watching a tall, slender young man move around the table, sizing up shots, working out angles. A few weeks from his eighteenth birthday, Joe should be revising for his A-levels, not playing snooker with his dad. He took some persuading, although not because he thought he should be revising. He's bright, bright enough to know what work ethic means, but that's as far as it goes. His mum and I worry about him, always have done. A fortnight ago she told me he wanted to go to a funeral and could I give him a lift? His friend Eddie, not a close friend, but still. Suicide.

'Joe,' I say, 'you're not using the chalk. Use the chalk.'

He screws up his face, curls his lip. His standard look for unwanted advice. But he picks up the chalk and chalks the end of his cue. His granddad's cue, I should say. Loosely between my fingers, as I wait for the chance to come to the table, I hold my own cue, which my dad bought me when I was about Joe's age.

'What happened?' I asked Joe as I drove him to Eddie's funeral.

'Dunno. He kind of withdrew over the last few months.'

'What did he…? I mean how…?'

'Overdose.'

I wondered about that word. Wasn't it what a professional might say? I wondered if this was what Eddie's parents said when anyone asked. *He took an overdose.* I wondered how they must be feeling, but shut down that line of enquiry pretty quickly.

I watch Joe stretch across the table to play a shot, one of his size 11 trainers planted on the floor, the other raised behind him, his leg straight as a rapier in baggy jogging pants. On his top half he's wearing one of my 90s long-sleeved T-shirts, which fits him better than it ever fitted me. Gone is the gangly awkwardness of youth, replaced by a fluid agility, latent strength, elegance. He handles my dad's cue with relaxed confidence. Now I know he can play – though I wonder when and where he learned – I'll tell him the cue is his to keep. I wonder if he's been watching the action from the Crucible on his laptop in his bedroom. It would make a change from Facebook or *Game of Thrones*. I wonder if other parents see more of their teenage children than I do of mine, or if they all stay holed up in their bedrooms.

When I picked him up after the funeral I asked how it had gone.

'Good.'

It seemed a strange word to use.

'Did you meet his parents? How were they?'

'Yeah. They were fine. His dad seemed quite cheerful.'

This made me wonder if Joe knew what was at stake, if he was able to empathise. If he thought Eddie's parents were 'fine' and Eddie's dad's cheerfulness anything other than a mask, might that mean he would be more likely to follow Eddie's example if some impulse told him to? Like I said, his mum and I have always worried.

He was staying at my place that night. After he went out, to the pub – it was a school night, but I guessed it counted as an exception, provided he was meeting a couple of mates to share memories of Eddie and not sitting on his own with a couple of pints – I wandered into his bedroom to pick up his clothes and generally tidy up and there on his bedside cabinet I saw the order of service for Eddie's funeral with what must have been a recent photograph of him on the front. Clear complexion, side-parted blond hair, a faintly disbelieving look in his eyes and an ambiguous half-smile, as if he'd just been told a bad joke. Inside I found the words to a hymn I didn't know, a psalm, a poem ('So Go and Run Free'), a reading by Eddie's dad, more prayers, recessional music by an artist I hadn't heard of. On the back, an invitation to join the family for refreshments. Donations, if desired, to Young Minds: Child and Adolescent Mental Health.

Joe is straighter on the black than he would have liked and will have to screw back hard to get on the red near the middle pocket.

'Shot,' I say, knocking twice on the floor with the butt of my cue.

Joe frowns. It's still a difficult shot into the middle, but he's steadily building up a decent break. I remember when my dad used to take me to the Chorlton Snooker Centre, neither of us could put together much of a sequence. A red and a colour – any colour – was about the limit.

He pockets the red and drops nicely on the blue.

I work out that when my dad and I used to play, he was only

ten or eleven years from the end of his life. We probably only went once or twice; my mum doesn't remember us going at all. 'Your dad would never have taken you there,' she insisted the other day. 'You signed the pledge, didn't you?' I said. 'Did you know the Chorlton Snooker Centre used to be the Temperance Billiards Hall?' But I remember him, as clear as day, standing in the half-light of the snooker hall, removing the jacket I'm wearing today and placing it on the nearest bench. He was my height, but stockier.

It's a good job Joe is keeping score. Left alone, he will sometimes get on with things. He's fiercely independent, except when it comes to loading a dishwasher or boiling a kettle. Would he take his parents' advice over exam revision, A-level choices, university applications? He would not. As a consequence he accepted only one offer, which is dependent on grades he's not predicted to achieve. Do we worry? Yes, his mum worries. I worry. Even my partner worries. I daresay his mum's partner worries, too.

I said to his mum the day after Eddie's funeral, 'Something like this puts things into perspective. We both know we worry about him. We've always worried about him. But at least he's healthy and happy. Nothing else matters.'

And if it were really the case, that my son was healthy and happy, nothing else would matter. But the vivid green of the baize is fading, the clink of the balls changing timbre. Doesn't it actually sound more like someone collecting empty glasses in a pub? Maybe a pub that was once a Temperance Billiards Hall and became a snooker club and now doesn't even have a pool table. The kind of pub where middle-aged men buy two pints when they visit the bar, then sit on their own at little round tables, sneaking occasional bites from sandwiches in paper bags. The kind of pub where you might go to sit and wonder what it must feel like to have your worries in perspective. What it must feel like to be the father of one of the boys at Eddie's funeral. A boy like Joe, perhaps. What it must feel like to be Joe's dad, and not Eddie's.

Salt

He's a nice guy and everything. Well, he's OK. But you can't help but look at his track record and wonder. One published novel, I don't know how many hidden away in the bottom drawer. And the one that *did* make it didn't *really* make it, if you know what I mean. Yes, it was published, but it didn't set the world alight and it's been out of print for donkey's years. No one on the course has read it or even seen a copy – except me. How can we take instruction from someone who doesn't seem to know how to do it himself?

Am I being harsh? After all, he's a published novelist. He didn't self-publish either; a proper publisher bought it and put it out because they thought it was good enough (or because they thought they could make money out of it, but having read it, I kind of doubt it). That's precisely what all of us on the course dream of, to have a novel published. It's weird how books are meant to be under threat from all other forms of entertainment and kids don't read any more and bookshops and publishers find it increasingly hard to make ends meet, yet everyone, from A-list actors to stand-up comedians to top poets to the woman down the street, everyone wants to write a bloody novel. And Dave, our course instructor, has done it and me and the other girls and our two token boys, who are really honorary girls since Vince is gay and Justin's so sweet it's like he's a girl, are all thinking big deal, so what, where's his second?

So, yeah, maybe I'm a bit hard on the guy. But you know what they say. Those who can, do; those who can't, teach. And that's a bugger of a sentence to punctuate. Not at all convinced I've got it right; Dave would know how to do it. One thing he does know about is punctuation. Use a semi-colon correctly and suddenly Dave's your best friend, until you confuse it's and its, or there and their. Whatever. Still, the argument goes, if he were any good, he wouldn't need to teach. Right? Wrong. Look at Martin Amis. The moment the 50-something *enfant terrible* of British letters announced his professorship at Manchester, hundreds of washed-up novelists in universities up and down the country received an ego boost the equivalent of Mariella Frostrup suddenly saying, in her gravelly voice, 'What we really need are more novels by X.' They felt validated. They were able to take that resignation letter out of the print queue. They even started thinking about getting stuck into another novel – or resurrecting the last failed attempt.

Dave's got all of that going on, I reckon. Anyway, I'm waiting outside his office for a quick meeting, not really a tutorial, I haven't got time for that, but, amazingly for me, I'm five minutes early, so I don't knock. Suddenly his door opens and one of the three people he shares his office with comes out and Dave sees me and gets up and suggests, since it's so busy in there, that we go to the canteen, which I'm cool with. So we head downstairs and he's moaning about not having his own office. Something to talk about, I guess. I nod and make appropriate noises, but I'm wondering if he knows I've read his book. How could he? I've not told him. I've been careful not to let it slip. I haven't even told any of the others I've got a copy, let alone lent it out. *Salt*, it was called, about a guy whose wife dies from eating too much salt. That may be an over-simplification, but that's basically it. He does go on about it, does labour a point, but when you factor in the research that's been done, a lot of it since he wrote his novel, about the dangers of consuming too much salt, it kind of makes it OK, I guess.

Dave gets a duck-breast wrap with hoisin sauce or something equally Daveish, while I get a plate of chips. I'm sprinkling them with salt when Dave says, 'Go easy. It'll kill you,' and that gives me a jolt, but when I look up, he's got this weird half-smile on his face. I think it's Dave's attempt at a full smile, but he doesn't really do smiling. There's too much seriousness and tragedy in that big balding head. Stretching a smile across it must seem a bit like sticking a smiley badge on the door to the mortuary.

'I was thinking,' I say to him, 'you know you told us all to write a horror story for Halloween?'

He nods.

'I'm struggling with it. I'm trying to experiment with point of view and perspective, like you said, and frankly the further I get into it, the less I feel I know about how it's all done, and I really need a tutorial, but I can't get away for long enough during working hours because of my job. Anyway, you once offered to make yourself available out of hours and I'm wondering if I can make an appointment, and probably not here, either, 'cause it's a right bastard to get to. Oh, excuse my French,' I add because I just looked up and he had this, like, bizarre look on his face and I'm thinking do I really want to book to see this guy out of hours? But I tell myself he's been checked and double-checked or else they wouldn't let him work here and I really must stop being so paranoid.

'No problem at all,' he says and I'm like, 'Cool, thanks.'

So, a few days later, I'm walking down his street in a leafy part of town. Leafy, perhaps, but not particularly well lit. The houses are all big semi-detached jobs with drives and front gardens and loads of brilliant hiding places for muggers and rapists, and I know what you're thinking. Why did he suggest we have the tutorial at his house, and more to the point, why did I agree? Look at the alternatives. Coffee shop? There's only Starbucks and obviously I'm not going there. We could hardly meet in a pub, because (a) it's a Friday night and we wouldn't get a seat and we'd be shouting at each other to make ourselves heard, and (b) it could easily, and weirdly, start to feel like a date, and from Dave's point of view especially, that has to be avoided. From mine too, of course, but I'm not the one who'd face awkward questions at work on Monday morning. Although, from what I've heard, it's not like Dave's colleagues – or perhaps I should say former colleagues – have been models of propriety where relations with students are concerned. But still. As far as I understand it, Dave's got family. That's what his biographical note says, anyway. Dave lives in Manchester with his family and teaches creative writing at blah blah blah. This is his first novel. It's a bit like saying, 'This is my first wife.'

The appointment was set for six o'clock. It's the best time of day, at this time of year, for having a nose in people's windows. Too early to close the curtains but dark enough to have the lights on, so all these comfortable reception rooms with their framed pictures and their well-stocked bookshelves, their dining tables and upright pianos, they're like little stage sets each one, shining under the lights. Most are empty, but now and again you see someone drift in and wander out again. Maybe they glance out into the darkness and see me, my ghostly white face hovering at the end of their drive like something painted by Edvard Munch.

Dave's house is near the end of the street. It's the one with the group of mannequins in the bedroom window. I'll admit they gave me a fright as I looked up. Nice one, Dave. One dummy in a window, OK, but three, and two of them children? Each to his own, Dave. I squeeze past the knackered old car in the drive and ring the bell.

Dave opens the door and we get through the pleasantries and small talk and I can hear myself overcompensating for my shyness and generally being a bit of an idiot, and Dave's trying to make me feel at ease, but he's not a terribly relaxed person himself and so he's not that good at it. We shuffle down his hall to the kitchen at the end and he says he was having a beer and would I like something and I say I'll just have a glass of water if he's got one. If he's got one? Like his taps might not be working. He pours me a glass from the fridge and we sit down at his kitchen table at a slight diagonal, as if that might be less weird than facing each other directly, but of course it's weirder, because when would you ever sit diagonally across from someone if there are just two of you?

'It's quiet round here,' I go, meaning the area generally, but I can see he thinks I mean his house.

'They're upstairs,' he says.

I look away because I can't meet his eyes and on the shelf alongside is this weird-looking lizardy thing.

'What's that?' I ask before I can stop myself.

'It's a mummified lizard,' he says. 'My sister brought it back from Egypt years ago. I like it.'

'You're into mummies, aren't you?' I go. 'I guess it's the salt.'

Too late, I've said it. I want that nice wooden kitchen floor to open up and let me fall into the cellar that is no doubt underneath. He's looking puzzled.

'They use salt, don't they, as a drying agent?' I say.

'And why…' he begins.

I'm cross at myself, but I'm also starting to feel a bit cross with him, too. Why should it have to be a secret that I've read his novel? It was published. Why wouldn't his students – or one of his students, at least – be interested enough to get a copy and read the damn thing?

'You read us that short-short story by Christopher Burns,' I said. '"The Mummification of Princess Anne". As an example, you said at the time, of a short-short that was actually worth writing, unlike all those Dave Eggers stories in the *Guardian Weekend*. Remember?'

'Of course. I'm just pleased *you* do.'

'It was great,' I say, overcompensating again. 'I'd love to reread it. What was it in again?'

'It was in an anthology called *New Stories 1*.'

'*New Stories 1*. I like that. It's confident. It's like saying, "This is my first wife."'

He looks at me, but I can't meet his eyes. I just want to die.

'I'll go and get it,' he says. 'You're welcome to borrow it. You strike me as someone who looks after books.'

He leaves the kitchen and while I listen to his footsteps going upstairs I find myself looking around, checking the table, the work surfaces, the island. I spot a pepper mill, but there's no sign of a salt cellar. I hear a muffled voice upstairs, but only one. I drain my glass and then he's back, with the book, which he puts on the table.

'Where's the nearest loo?' I ask. 'Weak bladder.'

'Downstairs. Just go out of the kitchen and turn right. The stairs are in front of you.'

I find the loo in the cellar. The seat is up. Hmm. I'm thinking this was a pretty terrible idea, coming to Dave's house, and I'm wondering how much worse it can get. Maybe there's another way out of the house from the cellar and I could escape and quit the course and give up writing and never have to see Dave ever again. Half with this in mind, although not seriously of course, and mainly because I'm a nosy cow, I check out the rest of the cellar. There's enough room down there for a student flatshare. I push open one door – it's already open really, I just have to open it a little bit wider – and see a couple of huge bags slumped against the wall. I see my hand reaching out to pull open the top of one of them to check out what's inside and I'm slightly weirded out to see that it's full of salt. Not table salt and you wouldn't want to cook with it, but salt all the same. Like the kind of salt they used to put on icy roads when you were a kid. Why's he got two great big bags of salt in his cellar? And why are his wife and kids so implausibly quiet? And then I hear his voice floating down the stairs from the hall.

'Are you all right down there?'

No, I'm thinking. Not really.

Strange Times

Strange times. Hope you are keeping well, anyway.

These are tough times for all of us, and it's important that we're looking out for one another. As MD of PizzaExpress, I wanted to update you about how we are planning to help our customers, teams and communities at this difficult time.

I decided to message everyone who was following me on Twitter to reconnect and say if you need anything from me – a chat, a virtual hug! – I'm here.

I am writing to people to keep contact in these strange times.

Welcome to Only Connect, a letter from the RSL coming to you three times a week (Monday, Wednesday and Friday), helping us to stay close to one another in these times of isolation.

Hope you are keeping well, and Happy Birthday for last week (though certainly strange times for a Birthday or pretty much anything).

Hope you and your family are all safe and well during these strange and difficult times.

Here for you during these difficult times.

Hope you are keeping well, and that things aren't getting on top of you. Thanks for the way you've all pitched in during these strange times.

Hope you're going ok with all the craziness.

Hope you and your family are well, and that your extensive book collection is keeping you sane during the trials of online teaching at this crazy time of year.

I hope you and yours are well, and managing without too much difficulty during these challenging times.

We value your support as a member of BTO, and hope that this is something that you might enjoy participating in during these difficult times.

I hope you, your family and friends are all well at this challenging time.

Just been out for a midnight stroll in the neighbourhood. Saw two humans and three foxes! Strange times indeed.

How are you? Hope you're doing Okay with all this.

I hope you and your family are keeping well and safe through these strange times we are living in?

Hope this finds you well in these strange circumstances.

Hope you are feeling well in these very strange times.

Just to say *The Mermaid of Black Conch* was published 3 weeks ago and is out swimming in the world during these difficult times.

I hope this email finds you well. In these unprecedented times. Adjusting to the new normal. Stay well.

Hope all's well with you. Obligatory mention of keeping safe in strange times (meant wholeheartedly, though).

I hope you are staying healthy and sane. I'm completely insane, at this point, oh well.

Hope you and your wife are keeping safe and well.

What strange times – are you doing ok?

In these very strange times what can be more welcome than a new Sparks album?

Hope you are okay at this strange time.

Hope you are well or as well as can be during these difficult times.

We hope that you are staying safe and well during these unprecedented times.

No one should have to face the coronavirus crisis and its devastating fallout alone. On Monday, we will discuss how we can support one another through this challenging time.

Hope you are bearing up in these weird times.

We're sorry that your recent order on AbeBooks was cancelled. Our sellers are working hard to fulfill orders for customers around the world during these unprecedented times.

I hope you're well in these very strange times!

Accurate and up-to-date records can save you time and help your business become more efficient, especially during these difficult times.

Meanwhile I wish you well in these difficult times. Take care and chin up!

Life here continues as best it can in these strange times.

Hope all well with you and you're surviving these strange times.

Hope you're faring well despite the latest restrictions.

I hope you and yours are staying safe and well and taking care of yourselves in these difficult times.

Hope you're well and 2020 with all of its strange events has treated you kindly so far!

A *coup de chapeau* for your funny, quirky, grainy Twitter chronicles. In these difficult times a special source of enjoyment.

I hope you're keeping well in these difficult times.

I really hope this finds you well, particularly so during strange times.

I hope this finds you safe and well during these strange times.

I hope this missive finds you well in these strange times.

I hope all is well with you in these weird times?

In these uncertain times, it's reassuring to know your money is in safe hands. So we wanted to remind you that as we're backed by HM Treasury, your savings are 100% secure.

Haven't been in touch for an age – hope things are OK with you in these far from easy times.

I hope all is well with you, your family and friends at this challenging time.

2020 was a difficult year for us all.

Hope you are doing OK-ish in these utterly shite times!

During this challenging time, we really need your help...

I hope this finds you well during this horrendous winter.

I hope you're keeping well in these strange times!

I hope you're keeping well at this difficult time.

I hope you are keeping well – what a weird time it is!

I hope you're as well as possible at this trying time – my thoughts have been with you all while we've been apart this last year.

Hope this finds you well and surviving in the world we are in...

Zulu Pond

I had gone out for a walk. I liked walking and it seemed the best way to reacquaint myself with the streets of the city I had known as a child. I crossed Fog Lane Park, then decided to cut through the housing estate, so turned right. I didn't catch the name of the street, but it wasn't important. There was a shop on the corner. There's always a shop on the corner. There were houses on both sides of the street. Identical box-like houses. Red bricks painted, for some reason, a deeper shade of red. Scarlet, perhaps. Cars parked on both sides of the road, up on the pavement. I heard the garbage truck before I saw it.

It was obvious it wasn't going to be able to squeeze through the gap between me and the car parked on the opposite side of the road, so I stood back and waited for the truck to pass. The vehicle was another deep shade of red. On the front were the words 'Manchester City Council'. There was another line of text to the effect that the truck was working on behalf of, or contracted by, the council. That made sense. Everything was subcontracted out these days. I also saw another word on the front of the cab: 'Alsiso'. The manufacturer, perhaps, or more likely the name of the firm contracted by the council.

The truck had stopped.

I looked into the cab, but the windscreen was reflecting a great slab of flat light, despite the lack of sunshine. It had been cloudy since I'd left the park. I beckoned the driver, indicating that there was room for him to get by. For a moment nothing happened, then the truck lurched forward and I caught a glimpse of three men sitting in a row, hi-vis vests, cigarettes jammed in mouths. The truck braked, then lunged. There was plenty of room, but the driver stamped on the brakes again and a door swung open. One of the men jumped down from the cab and walked towards me.

'All right?' I started to say, but he came right up to me and grabbed me with both hands, picking me up in one swift movement. He carried me round to the back of the truck; I tried to break free, but his grip was strong.

'Put me down. *Put me down.*'

Instead, he lifted me over his head and threw me into the back of the truck.

I landed in a heap of garbage among slippery remains of half-eaten dinners and the sharp corners of discarded yoghurt pots and the lethal edges of empty tin cans. I became aware that I was slipping lower down and instantly I recalled the way such vehicles were constructed, the way they compressed the rubbish they picked up so they could fit a lot into one truck. I heard the mechanism engage. The light was draining away. Something held me fast. I think I screamed. Or started to scream.

It was the scream – or the attempt to scream – that woke me up. And woke Jayne up.

'What's the matter?' she said.

'I don't know,' I said, dazed. 'A dream. A nightmare.'

'It's over now,' she said, her tone adrift between reassuring and impatient. 'Go back to sleep.'

Like that was a good idea.

I pulled on my dressing gown and went downstairs. In the kitchen of our tiny rented house, I filled the kettle and pressed play on the stereo. Drum and bass, in that order, followed by a simple, repeated guitar riff and finally the most haunted sound ever to come out of Stretford – the voice of Ian Curtis. Joy Division – the one band you could rely on not to try to kid you the world was better than your nightmares. I lowered the volume and sat down at the kitchen table.

The time was 4.10 a.m.

I stopped and watched the heron because I thought it wasn't real and wanted to prove myself wrong. It was perched on a wooden stump that rose six inches above the surface of the canal. I was passing by, cutting down Auburn Street on my way to a gig by the Fall at a club venue in Piccadilly, and a break in the wall on my left allowed a good view of the silent, green Rochdale Canal. The heron drew my eye, statuesque on a stump at the far side of the waterway. I watched for the tiniest movement, as it breathed perhaps, an infinitesimal rise of its grey chest, but couldn't detect even as little as that, so I leaned on the wall and waited, the night settling around me. Two couples crossed the street behind me, high heels beating a tinny tattoo, shushed by the melancholy owl's hoot of a tram. Still the heron didn't move. Was it a joke, a stuffed bird? Was it public art?

I remembered my dream of the night before. Quite apart from the horror of being tossed in the back of the truck, I was puzzled by the combination of plausible detail and the single unknown word – 'Alsiso' – on the front of the vehicle. I had once dreamt of a bicycle with the word 'GRAVLAX' stencilled on the frame as if it were the brand or model. I'd never figured that one out.

Below me on the tow path a white head appeared. A shift worker on his way to one of the multi-storey car parks beyond Deansgate. Sports bag slung over his shoulder, ham sandwiches and a Thermos. He stood as still as the heron, watching it. Like me, he wanted to see it move, wanted to know it was genuine. At the same time he, again like me, wanted it to retain its stillness, because there was something unreal about it, something miraculous, and it thrilled him to be in the presence of the miraculous. After five minutes the man reluctantly moved on, slowly, looking back as he went. He stopped at a point beyond which he would have been unable to see the heron, and looked back one final time. Still the bird hadn't moved. I watched as the man walked off under the next bridge.

I looked at the heron again and my heart stopped. Slowly the creature was moving its head forward, its impossibly long neck unspooling like celluloid tumbling from a reel. It moved a foot or so, no more than eighteen inches, then refroze. I breathed out.

I walked to the venue. It was a beer cellar. Stone flags on the floor. Flat-topped barrels dotted about for empty glasses. When the band came on they were only half an hour late. They looked surprisingly young, apart from Mark E Smith, who looked as if he should have been lying down. In a box. There was a fresh shaving cut on his cheek. When he wasn't singing, his jaw worked incessantly. I wondered if it was chewing gum, or bile. The sound mix rendered his vocals unintelligible, but the band were very tight and coped good-humouredly with Smith's stumbling backwards into the bass player; with his leaving his mic dangling over the guitarist's amp to create a howl of feedback; with, when a song had gone on long enough, his turning his back on the crowd and drawing his finger across his throat.

A lot of the material was new or from albums I hadn't heard, but it didn't matter. I was standing to the left of the stage close to the front, right by a speaker stack. Two yards to my right, the hard core erupted when they recognised the opening riff of 'Mr Pharmacist', bouncing, leaping, sprawling, a sea of bodies. At the front, bent double over the edge of the stage when the crowd behind him surged forward, was a Japanese student with a strange blond busby of dyed hair. He was too young even to have been born when I'd heard my first sessions by the Fall on the John Peel show. 'Slates', 'Middlemass', 'Older Lover'. They played none of those in the Bierkeller. The student, who had been sitting with his back against the stage waiting for the band to come on, so keen had he been to be right at the front, nodded his head, held his ground. Something seemed to insulate him from the physical threat of the moshpit behind him.

The band waited fifteen minutes before returning for an encore. The drunkest, boldest fan near the front grabbed a mic from the stage and bellowed, 'Come on, Smith, you ugly cunt,' to a cheer from the crowd, before a bouncer relieved him of it. Finally, the band filed back and did another couple of numbers, at the end of which they departed the stage in turn, following Smith's lead. Soon only the guitarist was left. He thrashed on for another minute or two.

Outside, my ears rang. The sound level had been higher than I had realised. The gig, like all decent gigs, had produced in me a sense of dissociation. While I could function sufficiently to cross Piccadilly, I wasn't really there. I was still in front of the speaker stack, the decibels pounding my ears, Smith working his jaw, enunciating one word out of every five.

I stopped at the break in the wall on Auburn Street, but the heron had gone. The water level, I noticed, had risen. The bird's perch was now below the surface.

In the car I fed the Fall's *Shift Work* into the CD player. I listened to a bit of the first track, but then ejected the disc and turned the stereo off before the radio could come on. Jayne would have left it tuned to Jazz FM. There was only so much smooth jazz I could take before being violently sick. That's right – none.

I put my hand in the door pocket and withdrew a fistful of CDs. Among them was *The Plateau Phase* by Crispy Ambulance. I'd been to see them the week before at the university. We'd only been back in Manchester two weeks and I'd already attended more gigs than I'd been to in London in as many years.

I looked in the rear-view mirror and drew my finger across my throat.

I drove home though wide, empty streets under regular lines of orange sodium lights. Beyond Withington there were more trees. By day they were filled with magpies and squirrels. As I turned into School Lane, a fox stood at the kerb. It wanted to cross, but I was approaching and there were two cars behind me. It changed its mind and turned away, trotting down the dirt path to the trackbed of the dismantled railway line.

The house was quiet when I got back, although my ears were still ringing. Jayne would have taken advantage of my absence to have an early night. I checked on Evie. She was lying across the bed, wearing pyjama trousers, her nightie and a cardigan. It wasn't cold in her room; that was just what she liked to do. In a box at the end of the bed she had lined up all her dolls, each in a sitting position. Her soft toys were in the bed with her. I managed to get the cardigan off her and she murmured as she rolled over. I switched on the bedside light, so I could see her face properly. People said she looked like Jayne. By people I mean Jayne's family. I couldn't see it, but I liked the idea that she should look like one of us, at least.

She'd celebrated her fourth birthday not long before the move.

I switched the light off and closed the door quietly behind me. I moved along the landing and pushed open the door to our bedroom and listened to the regular sound of Jayne's breathing. She appeared to be deeply asleep. I pulled the door to and went downstairs. I looked through the CDs that hadn't been put into storage. Since being back in Manchester, I'd been listening mainly to Manchester bands, as if to help me reacclimatise. It was Jayne, though, who pointed out, while she was looking for something a bit different to put on one night, that there was no choice.

'It's all miserable 80s stuff,' she said. 'Which reminds me. Miggy phoned. I said you'd call him back.'

I didn't react to the news that Miggy had called. As for Jayne's observation about the limited range of CDs, I couldn't argue with it. It seemed as though, when deciding what to bring to our rented house and what could go into storage, I'd pretty much narrowed down the field to what I'd listened to when I last lived in the city. I'd noticed, while driving around at night, that if I played anything originating from elsewhere it didn't sound right. Maybe going back anywhere would have the same effect. Or maybe it was Manchester.

Or maybe it was me.

We went to look at a house. Houses in Didsbury tended to sell within a few days of going on the market. Vendors could charge what they wanted. Offering less than the asking price was a waste of everyone's time. The best houses ended up going to sealed bids. It wasn't what Jayne had been expecting, moving up from London.

The rented house was temporary, while we looked for somewhere to buy.

Everything was temporary, I pointed out. Buying is just the same as renting, really. You only end up getting rid of it eventually. Or it – life – gets rid of you.

'The difference is the money,' Jayne explained.

I didn't understand money. That was her point.

The house was in Withington, but within a few months it would be in Didsbury, following a proposed boundary change. I drew alongside and pulled on the handbrake.

'The house next door is double-fronted,' Jayne remarked.

Normally it would have been me accentuating the negative.

'They're Cheshire semis,' I said.

I hadn't noticed this when looking at the details. If I had, I might not have agreed to view the property.

'What's a Cheshire semi?' she asked.

'It sounds like one of those jokes, doesn't it? What's a Greek urn?'

'Are you going to tell me?'

'Five hundred drachmas a week.'

Jayne reached for her door handle. I placed my hand on her arm.

'A Cheshire semi,' I said, 'is one where one of the houses is double-fronted and the other, its neighbour, is single-fronted, but double-backed.'

'How does that work?'

'Internally, the dividing line between the two properties is cocked.'

Jayne considered this, trying to picture the layout.

'You'll see when we get in there,' I said.

'Why are they called Cheshire semis in Manchester?'

'Perfectly reasonable question,' I said.

But Jayne had already climbed out of the car and closed her door on the end of my response.

The vendor was a music teacher at the Royal Northern. He told us he'd been there twenty years. I asked him if he'd known Dick Witts of the Passage, who had studied at the college. Andy Wilson, also of the Passage, had been in my class at school. The vendor said the name didn't ring any bells. He asked us what we did.

'I'm a barrister,' Jayne told him. 'My chambers wanted to open a Manchester office.'

Jayne was looking at the chandeliers in the hall.

The vendor looked at me.

'I don't contribute much,' I said. 'I'm a musician.'

'Musicians contribute a great deal,' the man said, but Jayne had already wandered into the main reception room. We – the music teacher and I – exchanged half-smiles.

'Where are you moving to?' I asked him.

'We're rattling around in this place,' he said. 'My wife and I. Our children have left home.'

Empty nesters. Most of the houses we'd looked at were being sold by empty nesters. Consequently, many hadn't been touched for fifteen years and needed new bathrooms, kitchens, the lot.

'I get the whole Cheshire semi thing,' Jayne announced, breezing out of the reception room at the rear. 'The house next door wouldn't have this room. It's like having an extra room. I like it.'

'If you don't get it in front,' the vendor said, 'you get it behind. The house doesn't look as big from the front, but it turns out to be deceptively large.'

'So the house next door, or its equivalent, is always going to be disappointing,' I said. 'Promising more than it delivers. Like life, really.'

'It's like you've got a secret room,' Jayne said, ignoring me. 'I like it.'

I didn't. Manchester already had enough history for me, enough secret stuff buried away. Hidden rooms at the backs of houses. Moments sinking in the quicksand of time.

'Do you need a house this big?' the vendor enquired doubtfully.

'We've got a little girl. She's at nursery,' I said. 'I work from home. And my wife needs a study, too.'

'It's a lovely house,' Jayne said, rejoining us.

It was, I suppose, but I couldn't see it. I couldn't see us living there. But could I see us living anywhere? It wasn't just self-pity, about my not contributing much. It was a real concern. I had been shocked by how literally my dream could be interpreted.

'Neil's from Manchester originally,' Jayne told the vendor.

'Really?' he said, leading the way down to the cellars.

'Yeah. You're a fisherman?' I said, spotting a basket and a rod bag in a corner.

'I haven't been fishing for years,' he said with a small sigh. 'Do you fish?'

'I did. Not since I left Manchester, though.'

'Maybe you'll take it up again?'

'You've certainly got the time,' Jayne interjected.

'I used to go every day in the summers,' I said, dodging Jayne's remark like it was a miscast line.

'Where did you fish?' the man asked.

'I lived in Altrincham, so King George's, the Bridgewater Canal...'

He nodded.

'Plus there was a little pond near the airport,' I added. 'Only a hundred yards from the perimeter fence, near one of the runways. You wouldn't know it. Nobody knew it.'

'You're right,' he said. 'I don't know it.'

'It was a secret place,' I said.

'How did you find it?' he asked.

'A friend told me about it. An acquaintance, really. Our window cleaner in Alty. He taught me how to make my own floats – floats were expensive – and he told me about the Crucian Pit. He said I could tell one other person about it, but no more.'

'But now you're telling me,' he said.

I looked at him, then over his shoulder to where Jayne was inspecting an old Belfast sink in the utility room.

'You're my one other person,' I lied. 'I never told anyone about it.'

The man in the Didsbury Village hardware shop greeted me and asked how he could help. I asked him for three metres of hosepipe and he asked me what thickness I needed. I said I didn't know and he showed me the range. I was surprised at the breadth of choice.

'You have a look, see what you need,' he said, 'while I serve this young lady. Yes, love?' He had moved back behind his counter. 'What can I get you?'

He was affable and helpful, no different from most shopkeepers I'd encountered, whether in Didsbury or in town. In fact, the only time I questioned the widely held view that Mancunians were friendly folk was when I went to pick Evie up from the nursery. Not only was I a new parent, or the parent of a new child, but I was possessed of a certain novelty value, being one of a small minority of fathers doing the picking up. I thought I might get a few smiles, perhaps the odd scrap of dialogue. But nothing. The mums chatted among themselves. The other dads seemed introverted. I smiled here and there, but the response was muted. Perhaps they'd heard how Evie had jumped the queue in the staggered start dates. If you don't ask, you don't get.

'We're going on a trip this afternoon,' I told Evie.

'Aw, I want to watch TV.'

'You can watch TV later. We're going for a little drive and then a walk, to see somewhere Daddy used to go when he was not much older than you are now.'

She seemed happy enough and demanded 'Cinematic Soul', the opening track on the latest Barry Adamson album, which had become Evie's in-car favourite.

We drove out of the village along Barlow Moor Road and turned left on to the Parkway. Within five minutes we were surrounded by farm land, Evie bursting with excitement at the sight of cows in a field.

I parked in a country lane off the A538 and opened the boot so I could leave my coat. Twenty years' living in London meant I didn't leave it on view inside the car.

'Daddy, what's that?' Evie asked.

I looked into the boot.

'Hosepipe,' I said.

'Why have you got hosepipe?'

I breathed in, looking at the three metres of coiled pipe, and out again.

'Don't worry about it,' I said, closing the boot.

We walked back towards the main road.

'Daddy, what's that?'

'Radar.'

'What's radar?'

'Come on, quickly, across the road.'

We climbed the steep embankment and I helped Evie over the fence. The hawthorn hedge was untidier than it had been a quarter of a century ago, but I recognised the scene: the smaller first field, which, like some kind of ante-chamber, had to be crossed before you reached the larger field where the Crucian

Pit lay hidden among nettles and willows. Evie and I walked through the long grass. I tried not to betray my nerves. The Crucian Pit had been special. I had felt privileged to be told about it in the first place and had kept the secret for a long time. Being a loner, that had been easy. I had no fishing mates. No one with whom to share the excitement of a tough little crucian carp tugging the rod this way and that as its golden flanks caught the sun even before I'd worked the fish to the surface. Two rod lengths across, thirty yards long, the Crucian Pit was twelve to fifteen feet deep in the middle. Crucians fight above their weight and you had to be careful, even with a small fish, to avoid having your tackle lost in the lily pads at one end, or the weeds at the other.

Evie and I climbed the second fence. In the larger field, we were more exposed. Anyone looking out of the windows of the radar station would have seen us. A security patrol on the other side of the wire fence a hundred yards away would have been on to us instantly. Twenty-five years earlier, you experienced a mild frisson at trespassing; after 9/11, for frisson read full-blown anxiety-inducing paranoia. Back then, your worst fear was an angry farmer. Now you imagined a squadron of black-balaclava'd SAS fighters appearing from nowhere, your face hitting the dirt, a knee between your shoulder blades. I wondered if having a four-year-old girl along for company made any difference.

'Daddy, these are nettles,' said Evie, as we picked our way towards the hidden pond.

'I know. Be careful.'

'They sting.'

'Yes.'

Maybe it would have been filled in.

It hadn't. But it was almost as bad.

The pond had been colonised by weed. I sat down on a little knoll and felt a sudden stabbing pain behind my eyes. I couldn't cry. Not here, not over this. Not in front of Evie. I stared at the surface of the pond like you might gaze at a stereogram, waiting for a pattern to emerge, something to give it meaning. I rolled my sleeve up and reached a hand into the water, pulling up a handful of weed. It was rooted to the bottom. I remembered the images from my *Angler's Mail* annuals of fishermen determined to clear a swim. They would tie the end of a rake to a length of rope and toss it in. Dragging the swim by retrieving the rake would remove the weeds. That sort of thing was fine for a stillwater that had become overgrown in the closed season, but I was looking at twenty-five years' accumulation of weed. Even if I dragged the entire pond, no fish could have survived that amount of build-up. A new ecosystem had replaced the old one.

Evie had wandered down to the water's edge. I watched her for a moment, then got to my feet. I approached her from behind as she dangled a stick among the weeds. I saw my hand nearing her shoulder and then settling on it.

'Daddy,' she said, turning round, 'you made me jump.'

I looked at her. The eyes round like unspoilt marbles pressed into the soft putty of her unlined face. The stud-like freckle on her earlobe. Mouthful of tiny perfect teeth. Well-defined nose, strong and straight. Then her face started to melt, as if there were a window between us and it had begun to rain. I pulled her into my arms and hugged her hard to smother my sobs.

'What's wrong, Dada? Dada?'

'Sh.' I stroked her hair. 'Nothing.'

When she started wriggling to get free, I broke off and buried my face in a tissue.

*

When we first announced we were moving to Manchester, people asked me if I still had lots of family and friends up there.

'Yes,' I would say, 'in Southern Cemetery.'

My dad and my great-uncle and my great-granddad were all buried there. My maternal grandparents had a memorial stone at the crem. As if by the law of averages, some of the boys I'd known at school had died, but, unusually, they had died while still at school. One lad was knocked off his bike by the 41X bus. Another walked through a plate glass window. One choked on his own vomit at a party. A friend with a promising career in band management ahead of him died at the wheel of a car. The only other boy from my year at primary school to go on to the same secondary school as me committed suicide by jumping out of an east London tower block after learning he was HIV positive, some five years after leaving school. I didn't actually know where any of these former acquaintances had been laid to rest. To tell the truth, their closeness to me had been enhanced in my mind by the very fact of their having died, and died so young.

I did, however, know where Miggy was buried. Right in the middle of Timperley, just off Park Road. Strictly speaking, Miggy wasn't dead. It just seemed like it. He lived in the house he'd grown up in. His father had died in the late 1990s, when Miggy had been living in London working for a record label. Miggy had gone up to Manchester for the funeral and not come back. His mother, who was already ill, went into a swift decline and followed Miggy's father into the grave within six months. Miggy's label had seized the opportunity to terminate his employment: they didn't do compassionate leave in the crisis-hit music business in the late 1990s. Not at Miggy's end of it, anyway.

Miggy hadn't owned his flat in London, so he just quit paying rent and moved what stuff he'd collected over the years back up to Manchester and tried to fit it into his old bedroom.

I parked in Leicester Avenue and walked to Miggy's gate. The house hadn't changed since his parents had died. In London, Miggy had been a live wire, always on the make, never satisfied. After his parents died within such a short time of each other, it was as if someone switched off Miggy's current. His parents hadn't been well off, but Miggy didn't have to work. He stopped going out. Some days he didn't bother to get up. Like most depressed people, he was too depressed to get help.

I pushed open the gate and walked up the path.

He opened the door in his dressing gown.

'Oh, it's you.'

'Get dressed, you lazy bastard. I'm not going to stare at your bollocks while we drink the tea I'm about to make.'

Miggy turned obediently and made for the stairs. If I'd talked to him like that in London, he'd have given as good.

His kitchen was disgusting. I did some superficial cleaning while the kettle boiled. Miggy reappeared in a pair of torn jeans and a prehistoric UK Subs T-shirt.

'I once saw Charlie Harper on Market Street,' I said. 'Asked for his autograph.'

We moved into his living room. I saw that not everything had remained untouched. A huge TV stood in the corner and there were stacks of DVDs on the floor.

'You know, it's been five years, Mig,' I said, when we were both sitting down. 'You can't just sit here and watch porn and never go out. You've got enough empty bottles in the kitchen to open your own recycling plant. You've got to pick your life up and get on with it.'

'Have you considered counselling as a career?'

'You're not the only one, Mig. My life's shit, too. Everybody's life is shit. What makes you so special that you can sit around playing with yourself all day?'

Slowly Miggy got to his feet and took a handful of DVDs off the top of the pile.

'*Later With Jools Holland*, Siouxsie and the Banshees, *The Old Grey Whistle Test*,' he read. 'If Whispering Bob Harris gives you the bone, you're even sadder than me.' He tossed them in my lap and sat down again. 'I get sent them. I do some reviews.'

I looked out of the window, then back at the DVDs.

'Is this any good?' I asked, picking out *The Seven Year Itch*, a live recording by Siouxsie and the Banshees.

''S'all right. If you don't care that she can't hit the high notes. In fact, it's not just the high notes, is it? But who gives a shit when she looks as good as she does?'

I smiled. Miggy smiled, too, if you could call it that. Although, if you hadn't seen Miggy for twenty years, you wouldn't have any trouble recognising him. He still had all his hair, a thick dark mop of it, unchanged in colour; his face was only a little fleshier, his cheeks still red as sweet English apples, his long straight nose somehow unscathed by alcohol.

'Things haven't turned out the way we thought they might,' I said.

'Got Alissa on your mind, have you?'

'Partly. I've been thinking about her, obviously, since we came back.' I got up and walked to the French window. 'Can you still get down there?' I asked, peering into the overgrown garden. 'To the pond.'

'Yes.'

'What do they call it? I can't remember.'

'They don't. It doesn't have a name.'

Miggy and I had met the night I met Alissa. The night she sang backing vocals for a local band, Performance, who were supporting Fad Gadget at the Squat on Devas Street. I'd gone on my own and was standing at the front when the lights

dimmed and Performance came on. They were remarkably together and confident for an unsigned band, and their material
was good, too. Melodic hooks and subtle harmonies, which was
where Alissa came into her own. With her kohl-rimmed panda
eyes and jet-black hair, she sucked the light into her face, which
bobbed like the moon at the back of the stage behind the five
other band members.

'Pip Crompton, Bernie Cox, Phil Walsh, Martin and
Stefan,' I recited.

'You what?' said Miggy.

'Performance. I never knew Martin and Stefan's surnames.'

'I didn't know any of their fucking names. I was there to
interview Fad Gadget.'

'Frank Tovey,' I said.

'What?'

'Fad Gadget. Frank Tovey. He died last year.'

'Fad Gadget?'

'Yeah. He was forty-five. Heart attack.'

'Fuck.'

We were both silent for a moment.

'I bought one of Performance's tapes,' I said. 'It had four
songs on it: "Janek", "The Next Train", "Baby Doll" and…
what was the other one?' I laughed. 'Does "Alsiso" mean anything to you?'

'No. Should it?'

'Dunno. Maybe. Maybe that's where it came from, although
it doesn't sound right.' I could see the trees around the pond at
the bottom of the garden. They were draped with magpies.
'I've still got the tape, you know. It still plays.'

'Yeah?' Miggy sounded bored.

'Look,' I said, pulling the tape out of my pocket and thrusting
it in his face. There was a Withington address typed on the label.

142

'Fuck off, Neil.'

'Shall I put it on? Do you want to hear it?'

'Not particularly.'

I'd spotted Miggy at the gig and latched on to him. I'd never seen anyone making notes at a gig before. It impressed me. He told me he was writing for a Liverpool fanzine called *Bop-eye* and that he had fixed up an interview with Fad Gadget. I asked him if I could tag along. I took his shrug for acquiescence and so followed him backstage when Performance were done. My legs were shaking so much I was relieved when someone invited us to sit down and offered us each a can of warm lager. Fad Gadget was busy getting into costume and so Miggy asked the Performance lads if he could do a little interview with them. They agreed and while Miggy started doing his thing, I realised I was sitting in the backing singer's seat. Her bag was on the floor next to me. At that point she suddenly appeared, emerging from a dark corridor at the back of the room.

I apologised and made to get up, but she put her hand on my arm and suggested I move along a bit.

'There's room enough for two,' she said, taking a pack of cigarettes out of her bag and putting one between her lips. She was going to drop the pack back into her bag, but had second thoughts and asked me if I wanted one. I didn't smoke, but I did want one, so I said yes. She lit it for me and sat down next to me, smelling strongly of make-up and sweat. I told her I loved the set, her contribution especially.

'That's sweet,' she said, blowing out a lungful of smoke. 'Tonight was a one-off. I usually sing with another group. But they asked me and, well, I just can't say no.' When she smiled at me, it was like she'd attached electrodes to me and flicked a switch.

I figured we were about the same age, but her confidence

was astonishing. This was her world. Singing in bands, going on the road, drinking, smoking. I took a deep swig of warm Carlsberg and an experimental puff on my cigarette. Coughing, I offered her the can.

'I'll get me own,' she said.

'I'll get it,' I said, reaching for another can from the cardboard tray that held them.

'Cheers.'

I knocked back another mouthful of beer, feeling it going to my head already.

'What's your name? Mine's Neil,' I said.

'Alissa.'

We were sitting on an old vinyl armchair. Alissa sat back and I upended my can. My thigh and upper arm burned where they touched hers. Someone tossed us two more cans and somehow we started kissing. Alissa got up.

'Follow me,' she said, and headed towards the dark corridor from which I'd seen her emerge back in what seemed to me like a previous life.

When we were both inside the toilet, she locked the door and turned the light off.

We couldn't have spent more than ten minutes in there, but for me it was as if time had stood still. I was aware, as Alissa stepped out of her dress and removed her bra, that this was a defining moment for me. The embarrassed, awkward fumblings in coat rooms at parties in Hale and Lymm and Warrington were behind me now. I was graduating to another level. A grainy blue light admitted by a little window allowed me to see gooseflesh advance across Alissa's body as my hand alighted on her arm.

When we left the toilet, the scene in the dressing room had changed. Everyone had left apart from the Performance bassist, who was stowing his instrument, and Miggy, who was deep in conversation with a girl I'd vaguely noticed hanging around.

'Where did you two disappear to?' he asked us.

We just smiled and then the four of us went back out to watch the main act. We continued drinking as Fad Gadget started swallowing his mic, ripping out tufts of pubic hair and pretending to attack his own hand with a power drill. When the lights went up at the end of an excellent gig, Miggy suggested we all go back to his house, as his parents were away and we could carry on partying as long as we liked. His battered Ford Escort was parked around the back of the Squat. It was fine by me. I'd left home earlier in the year, before my parents moved out of the region. I rented a bedsit on Palatine Road.

Miggy's friend, Rebecca, sat in the front passenger seat, allowing Alissa and me to spread out in the back, but it didn't take long to get to Timperley, not at the speed Miggy was going.

Rebecca didn't last long, passing out in Miggy's lounge. He opened the French window and the three of us entered the garden. Miggy had rolled a joint, which he passed around. He had some dried mushrooms lying around, too.

At the bottom of Miggy's garden was a big pond, seventy-five yards by twenty-five. It wasn't in Miggy's garden, but could be reached by passing through a gate at the bottom of the garden. The pond was entirely enclosed by houses, those on Leicester Avenue, Gerrard Avenue and Acresfield Road. Access to it was restricted to those homeowners whose gardens backed on to the pond. No other access was possible.

'It's a secret pond,' I said.

Miggy grinned in the moonlight. Alissa was swaying in time to some song in her head.

'It's like the Crucian Pit, I said.'

'What's the Crucian Pit?' asked Miggy.

I told him.

'Fucking hell! Right next to the airport?' he said.

'Practically on the runway.'

'You've got to fucking take me there,' he ordered.

'You can find it. You can go any time. It's easy,' I said. 'I'll tell you where to go.'

'You've got to fucking take me there now,' he said, grabbing me by the arms. 'I collect secret ponds. Don't you see? I need it for my *collection*.'

I laughed, but he was serious. His eyes were huge, sweat oozing from gaping pores on his nose.

'What about Alissa and Rebecca?' I said.

He looked at Alissa, who was smoking a cigarette and gazing into the pond, in a world of her own.

'They'll be fine. We'll only be half an hour. Ten minutes to get down there, this time of night.'

'It's a secret place,' I told him again. 'I'm only allowed to tell one person about it.'

'And you've told me. Don't worry about the girls. They'll wait.'

I told Alissa we were going out to get more alcohol.

Miggy advised her to come back to the house and wait there. He closed the little gate and we trooped up the lawn. In the lounge, Rebecca was still passed out on the settee. Alissa told us not to be long, but she was doing a good impression of the most relaxed person I'd ever seen. And the most gorgeous.

'Come on,' Miggy said.

'See you later,' I said to Alissa.

Miggy locked the front door after us.

'Just to be safe,' he said.

Twenty years later, I stood at the French window in Miggy's lounge and pressed my forehead against the glass.

'We should never have gone to the Crucian Pit that night,' I said.

'Statement of the bleeding obvious,' said Miggy.

I remember very little of our visit to the Crucian Pit. Miggy, who of course shouldn't have been driving, got us down there in about ten minutes, as good as his word. I don't know how we made it up the embankment, over the fences and through the nettles without sustaining any injuries. I remember Miggy's upturned face, his somehow appearing to eat the moon's reflection from the surface of the water, and a period of relative calm as we clung by our fingertips to the perimeter fence and gazed at the cones of shining moisture suspended over the taxiway.

When we got back to Miggy's house, Rebecca was still fast asleep in the lounge, but there was no sign of Alissa. The back door was ajar, so we wandered down the garden and found the little gate to the pond standing open. Miggy's various neighbours made their own arrangements with regard to security, but most kept their fences and gates low, allowing good views of the pond while still providing some protection for young children. Alissa could have climbed over any of them. One or two of the gardens that backed on to the pond even offered routes around the side of the owner's house direct to the street, without a locked gate. There were about a dozen different escape routes, and half of those would not have required anybody to be woken up in the middle of the night.

'How deep is it?' I asked him, gazing at the black surface of the pond.

'Deep,' he said. 'It's a marl pit. Lots of silt on the bottom. Slippery around the edge, too.'

It wasn't long after that that I met Jayne. She was studying at the university. We started going out. She met Miggy and seemed quite entertained by him.

I often thought life would be easier if I cut off all contact with Miggy, but for some reason I couldn't. We never reported Alissa's disappearance to the police. The pond was never dragged. I didn't know Alissa's surname, so I couldn't look her up. As for Rebecca, Miggy had given her a lift home in the morning. She'd claimed to have no recollection of anything that had happened since arriving at the Squat the night before.

I played the Performance tape over and over again, rereading the Withington address on the label, but knew I couldn't make contact. I walked by a couple of times, hoping for a glimpse of Alissa. The house was a Cheshire semi, divided up into flats. None of the names on cards posted by the bells was familiar. I asked in record shops. I pored over *Sounds* and *NME*. Some months later a single was released: 'Sensation Extension (I Need)'. I liked it less than the four songs on the tape. The B-side, 'Sandman', was better. Neither track featured a female backing vocalist. As Alissa had said, her appearance with the band at the Squat had been a one-off.

When Jayne graduated, we moved to London and I thought I'd probably lose touch with Miggy at last. But he popped up in the Smoke a year or two later and we saw each other every now and then. We talked about that night less and less. When the internet came along, I searched for a mention of Performance and found none. Every time a new band was launched with a girl singer, I checked them out in hope. But I never saw Alissa again.

I opened Miggy's French window and stepped into the wilderness that was his garden. The gate at the bottom was warped and wouldn't budge, so I just climbed over and there was the pond before me. The grassy bank that ran around the edge was covered with fallen leaves from plane, sycamore and beech trees. Miggy appeared alongside me.

'How come it doesn't have a name?' I asked him.

'Just doesn't. I guess because it's private. But even on old maps it's not named. It just says "Pond". Some of the locals have their own names for it. Bloke down the road calls it Zulu Pond.'

'Zulu Pond? Why?'

'It's his favourite film,' Miggy said, with a shake of his head.

'Has it ever been drained?' I asked.

'Not that I'm aware of.'

'What about this summer? The drought?'

'It's spring-fed. The level's gone down this summer, but only by a few inches. Someone installed a pump to combat the build-up of duckweed. There used to be a lot more water in this part of Timperley a hundred years ago or so. The other ponds were all filled in.'

'Any talk of this being filled in?'

Miggy shook his head. 'This lot wouldn't hear of it.' He indicated the gardens backing on to the pond. 'They've been here all their lives, some of them. No one sells up. I mean, you wouldn't, would you? They just sit it out.'

We went back into Miggy's house and sat in silence.

'You can't go on like this,' I said at length.

'At the risk of repeating yourself,' he snapped. 'Anyway, neither can you.'

I looked at him and he held my gaze for a moment before looking away.

'No,' I said, 'you're right.'

There was a long silence.

'Well,' I said, 'it's been lovely, but I have to go.'

Miggy grunted.

At the front door, I said, 'We may not see each other again.'

'I'll look forward to it,' said Miggy.

I walked down his drive, climbed into my car and switched on the engine. Just before the junction with Park Road, I pulled over: right for Altrincham and the route I used to cycle to the Crucian Pit, or left for home. I sat there for a long time, unable to decide.

The Lancashire Fusilier

There are some things you never wash. Leather gloves, certain types of hat. Scarves. Your mam never washed your scarf, did she? I'm glad.

This scarf? Never seen a washing machine.

Some of these other guys are here all day – morning, noon and night. Not me. I come when the Boat Train's due. The Harwich Boat Train. That's Harwich, Essex, not Horwich, Lancs. Two o'clock the Boat Train leaves – or used to. All right, sometimes I stick around a bit longer. I'd come every day in the summer, when there was no school. During half-term. In the Christmas holidays. I'd bring hot soup. The number of flasks I left here, sitting on a mail trolley, watching the trains. They'd be gone the next day and my mam would say she'd take it out of my spends, but she never did. What became of those flasks with their inner crust of congealed soup remains? Did they get shoved on the trains with the mail bags and end up in London, Plymouth, Aberdeen? These days they wouldn't last five minutes. Please do not leave your luggage unattended. Unattended luggage may be removed or destroyed by the security services. A secure left-luggage facility can be found on platform 10 to enable customers to store their luggage.

In those days the Boat Train was pulled by a Peak, a beautiful big blue bruiser of a diesel with a snub yellow snout, Class 45 or 46, sometimes even a 44, though I never saw one of them at Piccadilly. Down at Skelton Junction perhaps, but not here. Over the years I copped all the 44s and most of the 46s and every 45 bar one – 45123. It was one of the named locomotives. *The Lancashire Fusilier*. Sometimes the drivers were friendly and you'd not only cop a loco, you'd cab it as well. They'd let you climb up and sit next to them. They all had the same white enamel tea flask and you'd make a mental note to look for your soup flask when you got back down on to the platform. Do you think they'd let you cab an engine today? No, me neither. And we all know why. Please do not leave your luggage unattended et cetera.

But you can't take down train numbers all your life. My friends grew out of it. Sometimes I'd be here with Dave Entwistle or John Wright or Phil Maddocks. Did Phil Maddocks spot trains? I can't remember. One by one they all grew out of it and I guess I did too. I filled my last notebook, put my 1978 *Locoshed Directory* at the back of a bookshelf somewhere. Crucially, though, I did keep it. And over the years, as I moved away and looked for a job and met your mam and got married, I still looked at trains. If I saw an 08 shunter or a Brush 2 or even a Deltic as my train dawdled past sidings outside Crewe, Glasgow or Doncaster, I'd write down the number on the back of an envelope and when I got home I'd sneak a look in my long out-of-date book and if it was a cop I'd feel a tiny flicker in my chest and I'd get a ruler and underline it. And then I'd return the book to the back of the shelf and not think of it again for months on end. But I never saw *The Lancashire Fusilier* and time went by and, after years of trying, your mam got pregnant and you were born, a little early, a little underweight, and we moved back up to the north-west because we thought it would be a better place to bring up a baby. You soon put on weight and you were a clever one too, cleverer than your dad, you must have taken after your mam, and when you used to sit and watch the news reports from Afghanistan your mam and I would look at each other and I would change the channel, but we lived in a small Lancashire town and while it was a decent place to bring up a kid it was no place to be a young man. There were no jobs or prospects – or decent summers. We bought you a warm woolly scarf – yellow it was – and you wore it every day. We should have had the sense to get out, at least come down to Manchester, or even head back down south, for your sake if not for ours, but either we couldn't afford it or there was never the opportunity and you went along to the recruitment office and they said they'd have you. It made you feel wanted, you said, and although that felt to us like the point of a bayonet we understood, and you spent some time getting trained up and then you were gone, into the depths of the Afghan winter, six-month tour of duty, supposedly: there was a roadside device. Please do not leave your luggage unattended. They sent us your scarf, which you hadn't been wearing. If you had been, there'd have been nothing left of it to send. The Lancashire Fusiliers disbanded a lifetime ago, but that's what you were, essentially, a Lancashire Fusilier, whatever the name of your regiment, and that's why I started coming back here, hoping to spot a locomotive that was scrapped in 1988 pulling a service that was axed not long after. Your mam makes me a flask of soup, like my mam used to do, and sometimes I remember to take it home.

The Apartment

It's not as if I never hear voices. Three young men live in the flat under mine, so of course I hear voices. But these voices sound as if they are coming from the floor above.

Radcliffe Court is in Rusholme, hidden away so effectively, between Appleby Lodge and the Brighton Grove allotments, you'd almost think someone wants to keep it a secret. From the second floor you can enjoy views of the Toast Rack and the grammar school. Only from the windows, though, as there are no balconies, unlike at Appleby Lodge. I would have liked a balcony. In fact, I would have liked a flat in Appleby Lodge, with its Moderne styling, its Grade II listing and its blue plaque for Sir John Barbirolli, but there weren't any for sale. There was one at Radcliffe Court and it had two bedrooms. I live alone and have no children, but what I do have is a lot of books, their number increasing all the time.

I've been watching a bad film about a socially awkward man who orders a sex doll and has it custom-made to resemble his colleague. Potentially interesting material, sadly wasted. I bought the DVD, from a charity shop, because the notes on the back made me think of the novel one of my students is writing. I thought she might find it useful, but watching the film it soon became clear to me that it would be wildly inappropriate to send it to her. Normally I recognise wildly inappropriate only when it's too late. Anyway, her novel is a lot better than the film.

The film is so bad, in fact, I was starting to nod off when I heard the voices. I pause the DVD and the voices continue. Toing and froing, soft and low, yet audible through the fabric of the building and sounding, as I say, very much as if they are coming down through my ceiling rather than up through my floor. Is it a man's voice and a woman's voice? Possibly. I can't be sure. They are not exactly raised; it is not an argument. I can't hear distinct words, despite listening, as I am by now, quite intently. After a few minutes I realise I've been listening to silence for a while. I give it a bit longer, but hear nothing more.

The problem with the voices sounding as though they come from the floor above is there isn't one. My flat is on the top floor.

I eject the DVD and return it to its case. Maybe I will finish it tomorrow, in spite of its not being very good. I dislike not finishing things.

In the morning I take my coffee outside and walk right around my block, seeing if there is any easy way up to the flat roof. There isn't. Nor is there anywhere in the communal gardens to sit down and drink my coffee. At Appleby Lodge they have chairs and benches and a great big weeping willow to sit under. We have nothing like that. I drink my coffee standing up and go back inside.

I stand in front of the mirror, feeling the glands in my neck. Normal, as far as I can tell. The doctor appeared to agree, but encouraged me to continue checking them. Like I need encouragement.

I get my backpack and leave the flat, crossing Wilmslow Road into Platt Fields Park. The backpack is empty, but won't be on my way back. I walk up Heald Place through Moss Side and cross Moss Lane East into Whitworth Park. I rarely pass Nate Lowman's bronze *Snowman* without stopping to consider it. From the mysteriously unsigned warning sign – 'Please do not climb on the sculpture. We do not want you to be injured' – to the lethally sharp point of the snowman's carrot nose and the plaintive, barely legible communication on the cartoon figure's message board – 'I'll be dead soon' – *Snowman* is a one-artwork festival of misdirection and miscommunication. It gives me more to think about than either Michael Lyons' disassembled filing cabinet piece, *Phalanx*, fifty yards down the path, or, beyond that, Christine Borland's *Hippocratic Tree*, apparently inspired by the steel skeleton supporting Hippocrates' tree on the island of Kos but more evocative of the piece of children's playground equipment it most closely resembles. Every time I pass its warning sign I want to amend it to read, 'Please do not climb on the climbing frame. We do not want you to be injured.'

In the corridor at work I pass my colleague Jo, who asks me if I have time for a coffee.

'Next time,' I tell her. 'I promise.'

'Yeah, right.'

The piles of books on and around my desk in the office are gradually getting smaller. After packing my bag, I sit for a few minutes and look out of the floor-to-ceiling window at the tiny figures moving purposefully up and down Oxford Road.

The most direct route back is via Curry Mile. Its sights and smells are appealing – you might cross the road in front of a gold-chrome vinyl-wrap Jaguar F-type or deep-pink metallic Bentley Mulsanne, to stand for a moment in invisible clouds of sweet-smelling smoke outside the hookah lounges – but the combination of congested pavements and busy cycle lanes is stressful. Still, I haven't checked out the Alexandria Library for a while. The mostly foreign-language bookshop is at the bottom end of that stretch of Wilmslow Road; they usually have some general second-hand stock in the boxes outside. I found one or two things there the first time I went. On this occasion I pick out a Paladin paperback, *Notes from Overground* by Tiresias, with a James Marsh cover. The pseudonym is intriguing, also the fact I can't immediately tell if it is fiction or non-fiction, plus I will buy anything with a James Marsh cover and I am kind of semi-seriously collecting Paladin paperbacks. If the name James Marsh doesn't mean anything to you, he did those William Trevor paperbacks for King Penguin in the 1980s, or you might have seen his album covers for Talk Talk in the same decade. He likes birds, and fish, and creating the suggestion of a face out of unusual elements.

The pain, under my jaw on the left side, is intermittent. Pain is too strong a word. A sensation was how I described it to the doctor. Like someone – or something – prodding me there. Sometimes it is closer to the ear. And sometimes it appears to be *in* the ear and feels more like a blocked ear than anything else, but the doctor looked inside my ear and said there was nothing to see apart from a small build-up of wax. I might try olive oil, she said. I'd tried olive oil – will those stains ever come out of my pillow case? – but I tried it again.

When I get home, it's to find an A4 envelope from the Radcliffe Court management company containing news of a proposal to build another floor of flats on top of the existing three floors. There are already about eighty flats; the management company is proposing to let developers build another twenty-five or so. The government recently made it easier for freeholders to develop similar properties by no longer requiring them to gain planning permission to extend upwards. We already learned, at the last Radcliffe Court AGM, which took place not long after I bought my flat, that there is some unspecified relationship, indeed overlap, between the freeholders and the management company. Now, with the management company informing us that developers have approached them with this plan, I wonder what kind of relationship – or overlap – might exist between the management company and the developers.

There is a letter describing the proposal and outlining its benefits to residents. As part of the development, amenities will be upgraded and lifts installed at the rear of each block. It is anticipated that the value of the existing flats will rise. Strangely, no mention is made of any expected inconvenience or disruption to residents during construction.

There are architects' renderings, each one an A3 spread in full-colour photo-realist style. I take these to my kitchen and lay them flat on the table, where the light is best, although of course it won't be as good if they build another floor on top of the opposite block. The first is a view from the middle of Brighton Grove showing the exterior of the front of the main block and part of the boundary wall and communal gardens. The other two are slightly different views of the main courtyard and garage block enclosed by the horseshoe-shaped main block of flats. These are views very similar to those I would be able to obtain from the rear of my flat in the smaller block at the back. All I would have to do would be to exit my flat by the back kitchen door and walk down the back stairs.

I do precisely this and, once down in the courtyard, take a photograph from each of the positions where the architect's photographer must have stood. Then I walk around to the front and out into Brighton Grove to take a shot from there.

Back in my kitchen, I compare the photographs and the

artist's impressions. Gone are the weeds along the front edge of the boundary wall, and the mature sycamore tree and the small holly, these trees replaced by clumps of some sort of ornamental grass. Small groups of people stand about, in T-shirts and shorts. Some of the young men wear baseball caps. One of them is speaking on a mobile phone. A young couple in sunglasses push a buggy along the path. Two large white cars – a BMW M3 and a Kia Sportage – appear to be in motion on the interior roads, though when I look closely I see that neither contains a driver and, oddly, from the position of the steering wheel, each appears to be left-hand drive. Their number plates are blanked out, as if in a TV documentary.

The views of the courtyard and rear of the main block reveal surprisingly uncluttered walls. The flats have the correct windows, with pleasingly convincing reflections of the flats in the small block opposite, where my flat is, where, in the real world, I am sitting in my kitchen studying these renderings, but no flues or downpipes. You can see the promised lifts, which have taken the place of the back stairs, also known, importantly, as fire escapes. The vibe among the residents in the courtyard is less summery, more formal: suits, jackets, trousers. A man in a suit with a shaved head speaks on a mobile phone while walking towards a woman with a ponytail stepping away from one of the glass lift shafts. Two men with hands in trouser pockets have a conversation next to a vintage green E-type Jaguar and another man regards the rear of his BMW, which is sticking out of his garage (which, like the garage two along, also with an open door and a car sticking out, appears to have been wired for interior lighting). The man is probably asking himself, for the hundredth time, why the developers have not replaced the garages with garages that are big enough for the kind of cars pictured in the architects' renderings. I watched a real-world neighbour struggling to fit her real-world Mini into her real-world garage and eventually give up, parking it in the real-world courtyard instead.

The man with the shaved head and the woman with the ponytail reappear in the other courtyard view, which shows the adjacent row of garages, again with two doors open and two SUV-size marques sticking out. The man and the woman, still walking towards each other while he carries on making his phone call, are close enough to the BMW whose snout is protruding from one of the garages to suggest that one of them is its owner. The E-type has been moved to this side of the courtyard and one of the men with his hands in his pockets is still having the same conversation, but his friend is now out of shot.

I get up from the kitchen table and look out of the window, reassured by the sight of downpipes and hoppers and boiler flues on the rear elevation of the flats across from me. I imagine the extra floor on top of the block, which is easy enough to do now that I've seen the renderings, which show the extra floor with cladding attached to it to suggest, I suppose, a downwards extension of the roof. The pitch will have been all about 'flow'.

I realise that a man's voice I was vaguely aware of and had imagined to be coming from outside my back kitchen door – maintenance teams and cleaners often come up the back stairs – is not actually coming from that direction at all, but from upstairs. So, from the roof, or from the kitchen of the flat above that doesn't exist – yet. I can't quite make out the words, just a rhythm, and there's only one voice, as if the speaker is on the phone, and as I listen, it seems to recede back into the general background hum of real-world neighbours, and trains the other side of Birchfields Road, and high-performance cars sniffing out rat-runs between Rusholme and Longsight.

I watch the second half of the sex doll film, which I didn't manage to get around to on the previous two evenings, when marking students' assignments seemed like a more enjoyable prospect. The film doesn't get any better; it gets a lot worse. At least, at eighty-four minutes, it's mercifully short and I am able to get an early night. I set something playing, by Harold Budd and John Foxx, and place my phone by the bed. I remain sitting up for a few moments listening to the rushing sound in my left ear competing with the ambient soundscape of Budd and Foxx. As usual, the only way to silence the tinnitus – if tinnitus it is – is to allow the left side of my head to sink into the pillow. I lie awake for a few minutes worrying about the rushing in my ear and the intermittent pain under my jaw and about how long it's taking for my ENT referral to come through.

I'm woken by a cry in the night. I lie on my side, eyes open in the dark, as if that will help me pinpoint the source of the next cry, should one come, which it does a moment later. I am often woken in the night by foxes, but I don't think this is foxes. For one thing, it seems to me, the cries are coming from above. They continue to come, with increasing frequency, and then stop, and I lie there trying and failing to get back to sleep. I probe my latest mouth ulcer with my tongue, as if by giving it attention I might make it go away. I try thinking about the last story I have to write for my next collection, mainly to try to stop myself thinking about whatever the problem is inside my head and/or neck. It doesn't work and as usual when I am woken in the night it takes me hours to get back to sleep and no sooner have I done so than my internal alarm clock wakes me up again – at 6 a.m., which seems to have become my natural waking-up time, even if I've barely slept the night before, since I shifted numerically from my mid fifties into my late fifties.

I walk across Platt Fields Park in the drizzle, feeling like a line from a Smiths song that wants to be a Joy Division lyric when it grows up. Every couple of minutes I lift my head so I can feel my glands. I think maybe I can feel something on the left side, but then the mouth ulcer is on the left side, so that will be a normal reaction. The body trying to heal itself. I wonder why the mind doesn't try to do the same. Do I really think that the changes I'm making in my life will have the desired effect? When I get back to Radcliffe Court, the boundary wall catches my eye. Have the weeds along the front edge been removed?

I spend the evening liking posts by members of the Radcliffe Court Facebook Group – no one seems to want the planned development to go ahead – and watching a considerably better film about a sex doll, *Airdoll*, by the Japanese director Kore-Eda Hirokazu, whose earlier film *After Life* I found strangely affecting.

It rains heavily in the night, so in the morning I avoid the desire path across the grass in Platt Fields Park.

At work I find that for once I'm not the only person in the office. Pre-pandemic, there would always be half a dozen people in; post-lockdown, I'm usually the only one, but won't be for much longer.

Jo is sitting at one of the hot desks. We say hello and I go to my own desk and start loading books into my backpack and she comes over.

'Not many to go,' she says.

'No, well, I haven't got *long* to go.'

She watches me pack.

'What if you forget some or run out of time or something?'

'I imagine someone will just stick them on the shelves,' I say, nodding towards the communal shelves on the far wall.

'But would you miss them?' she asks. 'Would you even know you'd left them behind?'

'I don't know,' I say, feeling my neck.

'What even *are* these?'

'Penguin Modern Classics,' I tell her. 'There are lots of different designs but these are my favourite. The Marber grid with Helvetica and that lovely green-grey spine and back cover.' I hold up a copy of Kafka's *The Castle* – the one with the cover that's a detail from De Chirico's *The Enigma of the Hour* – to show her what I mean.

'Right. I saw a load of those in a box.'

'Where?' I ask her.

'Walker building, third or fourth floor. It was just, like, a box outside someone's room. You know, like when they want people to help themselves. Fourth floor, I think.'

It's my turn to say, 'Right.' I add: 'My dad used to hate that.'

'What?'

'People saying "right" all the time like that. He thought it was meaningless.'

'Right.'

'Right.'

There's a pause.

'Are you all right?' she asks. 'You look tired.'

'I'm not sleeping well,' I say. 'I'm being haunted.'

'Who by?'

I put three more books in my backpack and test the weight.

'Ghosts from the future,' I say. 'Having sex.'

'What?'

'Never mind.' I zip up the backpack. 'I'd better get off.'

'You've only just arrived.'

'I'm only really coming in to sort these books out.'

'You said next time we coincided we could get a coffee or something, have more of a chat.'

'Did I? Sorry. Can't today.'

'You're so unreliable.'

'I know.'

'Right.'

'Right.'

She puts her head on one side, looking at me quizzically.

'What?' I say.

'Have you lost weight?' she asks.

'What?'

'You look like you've lost weight.'

'I've got to go.'

I walk past the hot desk where her laptop screen displays a Word document and a paragraph of text in too small a point size to read without it being obvious what I'm doing.

When I leave the building I can go left or right. Right will take me past the Walker building. I go right.

Why have I never been in the Walker building? It's relatively new and is home to departments I have nothing to do with. Physiotherapy, psychology, sociology. Nursing. Like all new buildings – it's the law – it has an atrium and lifts with glass doors, not unlike the glass lifts they want to install at Radcliffe Court, except these ones are not enclosed by a lift shaft, not even a glass lift shaft. I walk in, the doors close behind me and I turn around to face the empty space of the atrium as I move up through it. The lift stops on the fourth floor and for a moment nothing happens, as if the lift is trying to decide which doors to open: those behind me, which will lead out – I presume, having never been here before – on to the safety of the fourth-floor lift lobby, or those in front of me, which would open on to a sixty-foot drop. A computer – or more likely a single chip – somewhere makes the right decision and opens the doors on to the landing.

I step into a dark corridor that lights up ahead of me in sections. Narrow windows in a series of doors all marked 'Clinical

Skills Room' reveal large interiors with picture windows in the far wall and hospital beds extending from that wall towards the middle of the room. In each bed lies a figure partially covered by a sheet, sometimes a blue blanket. Heads, shoulders, perhaps chests uncovered. Arms under or on top of the bedding. The figures lie on their backs, some with eyes open, others closed. Mouths also open, or closed, but a sense of either one state or the other, no shifting between. Faces somehow expressing need, alarm, desire, hunger. They want something but have no voice. Most are white, but some are Black. A Black male in a dark blue T-shirt, arms rigid by his side, mouth open a little, stretched in a wide rictus across his face. His bed is propped, allowing his eyes to meet mine. He looks caught between terror and confusion.

I try the door. It's locked.

I try other doors. They are all locked.

I pass through a set of double doors into a continuation of the same long corridor. A door marked 'High Fidelity Simulation Room' stands open. Lights on inside. This room is smaller with just one bed containing a figure with white skin and dark brown painted hair and eyebrows. His mouth is open, eyes closed. There is a drip stand by the bed, but he is not connected to it. The shape of his legs under the blue blanket. His feet sticking up. He looks dead rather than inanimate. The wall across from me is given over to a two-way mirror, in which I see myself – and the dummy in the bed – reflected. I wonder who might be on the other side of the two-way mirror. I back out of the room, watching myself.

I return to the lift landing, where there are also stairs going down.

The third floor has fewer of the large rooms and they are filled not with hospital beds but physiotherapy plinths and treatment tables. In place of lifelike dummies are small groups of upright skeletons on wheeled stands. An entire corridor is lined with grey doors designated either 'Experimental Testing' or 'Psychology Laboratory'. Given the number of doors and the short distances between them, they must be very small laboratories. I have seen no sign yet of a box of books anywhere. I turn a corner into a longer corridor. On the right are store rooms with narrow windows in their doors and what I presume are offices behind numbered, otherwise anonymous, unglazed doors. On the left are more offices, a staff kitchen, a 'Group Room', yet more offices. Then a door marked 'Control Room'. Only two doors remain between this and the end of the corridor. The first one is the same grey as all the other doors, but in a different style. It's a standard six-panel door like the door to a house or flat, the door to a home. A small sign has the words 'The Apartment' written on it in marker pen. The last door in the corridor, like the one before the Apartment, is another 'Control Room'.

I go back to the Apartment, look up and down the corridor, and try the door.

It's locked.

At Radcliffe Court a young man in a baseball cap is standing by one of the rows of garages talking on a mobile phone. I don't recognise him, but a number of the flats are owned by absentee landlords and rented out to students and young professionals, so there's a high turnover of residents.

I think about emailing Jo to tell her that I found the box of books, around the corner from the Apartment, and they were not the type of Penguin Modern Classics I collect, but I am distracted by an email from my student – the one writing the novel about the doll – who has sent me her latest chapters. I print them off and spend the evening reading these and eating cheese and drinking strong Belgian beer and vaguely listening out for voices from above and feeling my neck and tugging at my ear. Maybe I shouldn't be surprised when I wake in the night needing to go to the bathroom and then don't manage to get straight back to sleep but lie there with my eyes open in the dark thinking about what's going on in my head. I lie on my left side and turn over on to my right, my right arm thrust up under the pillow, then I retrieve it when I feel it starting to go to sleep, even if *I* can't, and turn to lie on my back with my arms by my side. I feel my mouth falling open and I think about Jo telling me I looked like I'd lost weight. It's the first question the doctor asks you. Have you lost weight? *Have* I lost weight? I should go and weigh myself in the bathroom, except that's the last thing I should do. Why did I not eat a proper meal? Have you lost your appetite? *Have* I lost my appetite? Should I get up and make toast? Eat more cheese. Put on weight. I feel my neck. I stick a finger in my right ear, pull on my left ear lobe and puff out my cheeks, trying to unblock my ear, not even knowing if I'm doing it right, but knowing I can't go online and look it up because of what else I might find. I can't live like this and yet I do live like this. It's no way to live. I reach over and touch my phone screen: 3.24 a.m. I turn on to my left side again so that I can't hear the rushing in my left ear and as I finally see coming towards me the line of trees, the edge of the forest, that I imagine represents sleep, I think I hear voices.

I wake again at 6 a.m. and run a bath and let it go cold and get dressed and eat toast and make coffee and drink it looking at the rear of the flats across from my kitchen. The hoppers, the downpipes, the flues – all still there. I get my backpack and head out. I look at the row of garages where I saw the man in the baseball cap. He's not there. No one is there. I walk across

Platt Fields Park, up Heald Place, into Whitworth Park. I leave the path and stand in front of the *Snowman*. I lean forwards until my forehead meets the sharp point of his nose. I stay like that for a moment, thinking that if someone were to rest a hand on the back of my head and apply pressure, probably just gentle pressure, it would all be much simpler.

I pull back and steady myself and regain the path, working my jaw as I make my way across the park.

I enter the Walker building and take the stairs to the fourth floor, where I walk down the same corridors and look through the same narrow windows into the same rooms and see— Are they the same dummies in the same positions or do some of them look different? Are there fewer Black dummies than yesterday? Have some of the male figures been replaced with female ones? Is one of the female dummies lying with her head slightly to one side? The white male with painted dark hair in the High Fidelity Simulation Room has been aged by the addition of a grey wig.

Even though there is only one long corridor of these Clinical Skills Rooms and Simulation Rooms, it seems as if the lines of beds go on for ever, filling corridor after corridor in my mind, an infinite space accommodating an inexhaustible supply of – what? Patients? Clients?

In the distance, a door bangs. Beyond the double doors, a man passes from one side of the corridor to the other. He will be going to the toilets. Exams are over, practical work surely mostly finished until the autumn, but some staff remain. *Someone* put the grey wig on the male in the Simulation Room.

I take the core stairs down to the third floor and head straight for the Apartment.

I try the door.

It's unlocked.

169

I look around. There is no one to be seen. I open the door and close it behind me.

With my back to the door, breathing quickly, alert, I see that I'm standing in a little vestibule. No sound comes from the parts of the interior that I cannot see. To my right is an area two metres square dominated by an Ikea coffee table with two small grey and red armchairs on one side and a grey sofa on the other. I move into this area and sit for a moment in one of the armchairs. On the coffee table is a paperback book, Frederick Forsyth's *The Fourth Protocol*. I pick it up and flick through it. The flyleaf reveals it was bought second-hand for £1. Towards the back of the book, at page 385, someone has inserted a quick crossword from the *Telegraph*, partially completed. They'd got 2 down, 'Boredom (5)', ENNUI, but not 8 across, which crosses it, 'Capital of Madeira (7)', and I realise I don't know the capital of Madeira either, so I wouldn't have got that, but I might have got ENNUI. I remember recently starting a story by Chekhov called 'A Boring Story', and not finishing it because I found it boring.

I put the crossword back in the book and the book back on the table and look up at the rest of the main room. Beyond the sofa is a small kitchen area. Table and four chairs, fitted kitchen, white goods. Windows facing north. Off the main room are a bedroom and a bathroom. The bed is made, curtains have been hung (more north-facing windows), a wardrobe stands empty, a folded ironing board next to it with a dressing gown draped over it. In the bathroom two signs state, 'Toilet not in use'. Bowl and cistern are both empty of water, but the basin and bath taps all work. Throughout the Apartment, the floor is covered in alternating grey and green carpet tiles. There are four CCTV cameras – three in the main room, one in the bedroom, none in the bathroom, but, in the bathroom, on the wall between the washbasin and the bath, a lowered roller blind conceals a two-way mirror. Another two-way mirror, also covered, is built into the bedroom wall, and in the main room the entire wall from the kitchen windows to the wall beyond which lies the corridor is taken up with floor-to-ceiling two-way mirrors. There are four roller blinds, but they are all rolled.

In the kitchen area there is a box of Tesco Special Flakes With Red Berries and a box of Asda Multigrain Hoops. Both contain small amounts of cereal. In the cupboards, boxes of Brunch Bars, an empty cake tin and a takeaway tub filled with sunflower seeds.

Back in the bedroom, I notice a line of books on the window ledge – Ian Rankin's *The Complaints*, Tony Parsons' *One For My Baby*, Kevin Lewis's *The Kid*, Frank McCourt's *Angela's Ashes*, a novelty book called *Why Don't Penguins' Feet Freeze?* for which the *New Scientist* appears to bear responsibility, and David Peace's *Nineteen Seventy Four*, a TV-tie-in edition that retitles the novel *Red Riding 1974* – and a selection of picture frames, some empty, others containing picture-postcard views. The view from the window is of trees in the foreground and the tops of the newly built towers of Deansgate Square beyond.

I hear footsteps in the corridor. I go to the door and listen as the footsteps fade away, then I open the door, see no one about, and slip out into the corridor. No one saw me enter the Apartment, or leave it, apart from whoever might be watching the CCTV.

On the way to the stairs, I pass Jo's box, which appears to be still full of the same unwanted books. On my way down the stairs, I put my hand to my neck and I realise that for all the time I was in the Apartment I did not once feel my neck. Nor did I hear the rushing in my ear or sense or think about the imagined blockage. Instead, for the first time in a long time,

I felt something close to excitement. I didn't know what the Apartment was, but I liked not knowing. I didn't even really mind feeling mildly anxious about the possibility of being challenged over what I was doing there. I'll take mild anxiety about something that's not a matter of life or death over severe anxiety about something that is, or could be, any time.

It's the weekend. The university will be closed. Plus, the new owners of Sharston Books, having been operating only online for some time, have decided to stop trading altogether. They have announced the shop will be open to visitors this weekend for the last time.

I walk south to the Mersey. The river meanders at this point, so I climb up to the level of Merseybank Playing Fields and cut across the green space. In the distance I see a man walking to and fro, back and forth, his body angled forwards. As I get nearer I see that he's walking in a circle and as I get nearer still I see that he's walking in an *existing* circle. He's following a circular path that's been worn in the grass, no more than fifteen or twenty metres in diameter, trudging around and around. He's wearing grey trainers and black running shorts and a blue sweatshirt with a broad white band. He has grey hair, must be late fifties, sixties. He looks down at the path as he walks, his face set, hard, a combination of wiry and jowly, inward looking, unwelcoming of an approach. I say, 'Hiya,' and receive no more than a grunt in reply. I walk past him and a short distance later come across another, slightly elongated circular path, like a miniature version of a running track, and then another, and it dawns on me, he's not just walking them – he created them. Later I will look at Google Maps, satellite view, and I will see that he has made seven or eight of these loops. He's like a land artist, an Andy Goldsworthy or a Robert

Smithson, and yet when I remember his dutiful trudge, his grim demeanour, I'm reminded more of Kafka's hunger artist or even the condemned man in 'In the Penal Colony'.

At Sharston Books I arrive to find the gates closed and locked. I see a woman walking between the main warehouse and one of the shipping containers that are full of books and I attract her attention. She uses her arms to indicate I should go around to another entrance. Once I get inside, I see that most of the shelves have been cleared. The classics, among which I might have found Chekhov's *Lady With Lapdog*, containing 'A Boring Story', have all gone. Behind the desk I find a young man playing on a phone. I ask him about the classics. 'All gone,' he says. I head back outside to look in the shipping container dedicated to fiction, where, on this last day, books are ten for a tenner. Many of the books in here are damp and have been damp as long as I've been coming here. If they're not damp they're covered in cobwebs or desiccated harvestmen or cellar spiders. I pick out David Leavitt's *Family Dancing* as it's a short story collection, Daphne Merkin's *Enchantment* and David Hughes's *But For Bunter* because they're both published by Paladin (and I like Merkin's name and the Hughes has been gnawed by mice and these seem to me like valid reasons for buying them). Christopher Kenworthy's *Will You Hold Me?*, another short story collection, at least two copies of which I already own but I can't bear for it to be pulped or go to landfill or whatever it is they are going to do with these books after today. Lewis Davies' *Tree of Crows* because it looks interesting but when I try to read it later I will find it's badly copy-edited and I will never finish it, in spite of what I said before about not finishing things. Frederick Forsyth's *The Fourth Protocol* because it's the same edition as the copy on the coffee table in the Apartment.

When I get these books back to Radcliffe Court, I clean the covers with a duster and furniture polish. I put the Frederick Forsyth on my coffee table, then I pick it up again and flick through it. There's no price marked in it and no *Telegraph* quick crossword at page 385. I put it back down again, then pick it up again and read the opening paragraph, which begins, 'The man in grey decided to take the Glen suite of diamonds at midnight. Provided they were still in the apartment safe and the occupants away.' I wonder if there shouldn't be another 'were' in there. 'Provided they were still in the apartment safe and the occupants were away.'

I feel a sharp pain under my jaw.

I hear voices. Indistinct, muffled, little more than a murmur.

I get my stepladders from the store cupboard outside the back kitchen door and fetch a glass from the draining board. I stand on top of the stepladders in the living room pressing the glass to the ceiling and my ear – my good ear, my right ear – to the glass, but the sound is no better. Well, maybe a little bit better, but I still can't hear what's being said. I put the glass and the stepladders away and stand looking out of the kitchen window. The flats across the way still look the way they always did. Nothing has changed.

On Sunday I walk to Chorlton. If I have lost weight, or I look like I've lost weight, it would be better to have a non-sinister reason for it, like I've started walking more, so I am going to increase my daily average. This way, I think, I will trick my mind into reducing my anxiety. Yeah, right, as Jo might say. In Chorlton's charity shops I find copies of Tony Parsons' *One For My Baby* and Frank McCourt's *Angela's Ashes*, both the same editions as in the Apartment. On the walk back I start reading the Tony Parsons and get as far as page ten: 'Sick and tired of trying to explain the glory and wonder of the English language to children who poured "fuck", "fucking" and "fucked" over their words like ketchup in a burger bar.' Where, in that analogy, are they pouring that ketchup exactly? Over their words? All over the burger bar itself? Shouldn't it be: '… like ketchup over a burger'?

Back at Radcliffe Court, I put both books on the window ledge in my bedroom. I get my own copy of David Peace's *Nineteen Seventy Four*, the 2000 paperback edition with Metl-Stik black-on-gold self-adhesive letters providing the cover artwork, and stick it next to them. I'll replace it with the TV tie-in edition if I come across one. This, for me, is the book that saves the Apartment bookshelf, because it's a masterpiece. Anything that gets that many one-star reviews and five-star reviews on Goodreads is likely to be and *Nineteen Seventy Four* actually is.

I fall asleep rereading the first chapter and am woken some time later by a bang and something like moaning. The moaning persists, unless it's the memory of my dream, or the rushing in my ear. There's another bang. I sit up in bed. My book is on the floor. Could that have been the bang, or one of them? Maybe there was only ever one. The bathroom door is closed – I usually leave it open because it can rattle in the frame if it's closed and there's a draught – and there's a window open inside the bathroom.

There's another bang, but this one is on the front door of my flat. I freeze and wait. Another bang. I move quietly out of the bathroom into the hall. I can see a line of light at the bottom of the front door, with two breaks in it.

'Hello?' I say.

Another bang on the door.

I get my key and unlock the door and open it.

'Mate,' says the young man standing there, one of the

young men from the flat below mine, I think. He's wearing a T-shirt and shorts. 'It's, like, the middle of the night. Can you not, like…'

'What?' I say.

'The noise,' he says. 'I don't like to complain, but, mate, you know what I mean?'

'There was a window open,' I say. 'I heard a bang. I didn't know what it was. I'm sorry.'

'Listen, fella. No offence, yeah, but sort the fucking noise out.'

He turns and heads back towards the stairs and I close and lock the door.

Platt Fields Park. Heald Place. Whitworth Park. Oxford Road.

When I get to the university, I see a young man in a baseball cap outside the Humanities building talking on a mobile phone. I stop and watch him for a moment. There are still some students around; he could be a student.

As I enter the office, Jo closes her laptop.

'Right,' she says, slipping her laptop into a shoulder bag. 'Let's get that coffee.'

I look at the remaining books on my desk.

'Let me just grab some of those,' I say.

'It's your last week,' she says as I open my backpack and see inside it the copy of Frederick Forsyth's *The Fourth Protocol* that I bought in Sharston Books. I must have put it in this morning when preparing to leave the flat. I select some of the books from my desk to add to it and then zip up my backpack.

We leave the office and go down in the lift. I get two coffees. There's no one else in the café.

'How do you feel?' Jo asks.

'What about?'

'Leaving. Your last week.'

'I'm on a deadline as well,' I say.

'Your story?' she says.

'I told you about that?'

She shrugs.

'I found the box of books,' I say.

'Any good?'

I explain about them not being the ones I collect but can tell she's not interested, so I tell her about the Apartment instead. Her eyes don't leave mine as I describe it to her. There's a half-smile on her lips.

'Sounds like you want to move in,' she says. 'How's your actual apartment, where you actually live?'

I tell her about the development plans and the architects' renderings and the banging in the night and the visit from one of the young men downstairs. I wonder if I'm telling her too much and break eye contact and look away out of the window. Outside, the young man in the baseball cap is walking up and down talking on his mobile phone.

'They call it "people texture",' she says.

'What's that?'

'The people in architects' renderings. Like you see on hoardings around construction sites where they're building luxury flats you can't afford. You know, like Deansgate Square and that.'

'People texture?'

'Yeah.'

I look out of the window again. She follows my eyes. We both look at the young man in the baseball cap.

'Don't you feel sometimes,' she says, 'like that's all we are?'

I look back at her. 'You *wanted* me to see the fourth floor, didn't you?' I say. 'In the Walker building?'

'What?' she says. 'Because it's some sort of metaphor? Like your people upstairs? Your so-called ghosts from the future?'

I feel myself frowning. 'And the third floor, for that matter,' I say. 'The Apartment.'

'We have to live in the meantime, don't we?' she says.

'Do we?'

When I press my nose up close to the two-way mirror in the main room of the Apartment, I can see through into the Control Room, which is filled with rows of seats, like a cross between a lecture theatre and a witness room attached to an execution chamber.

I think about being a student sitting in there watching a drama unfold in here.

I think about being a student on this side of the two-way mirror, aware that your every moment is being observed.

If you look up 'two-way mirror', it tells you that a synonym for it is 'one-way mirror'. If you look up 'one-way mirror', it tells you, not surprisingly, that a synonym for it is 'two-way mirror'.

I see the copy of *The Fourth Protocol* on the table and reach for my backpack. I take out of it the same edition of the same book from Sharston Books and place it on the table next to the Apartment's copy. The Apartment's copy is on the left, my copy on the right. I align them neatly and then sit back in the armchair and think about the fact that, perhaps because of the coffee I had with Jo, I need to use the bathroom. I look around at my backpack and the two books on the table. I leave them there and leave the backpack on the floor next to the armchair and cross over to the door. I press my ear to the door and listen, but can't hear anything, so open the door and look out. I step out, allowing the door to close behind me, and walk down the corridor to the double doors. The toilets are just beyond the double doors.

I pass back through the double doors and return to the Apartment. I open the door and go in and sit not in the armchair but on the sofa. I take my shoes off and bring my feet up on to the sofa and curl up.

A noise wakes me and I sit up, disorientated. It takes me a moment to work out where I am. I try to process the noise retrospectively. It could have been a door closing. It could have been someone knocking on the door to the Apartment. It could have been any number of things. I put my shoes on and go around to the other side of the table. Of the two copies of the same book I take the one on the left and put it in my backpack and go to stand by the door. I listen, open the door and step out into the corridor.

Curry Mile is busy. It's always busy; it's busier than usual. The traffic grinds along Wilmslow Road. A Range Rover crosses the junction with Great Western Street. Is it just the sun's glare reflected in the windscreen that makes it appear driverless?

At Radcliffe Court I have to walk around a Lexus and an Audi parked alongside each other outside the garages. As I approach my block, a young couple come around the corner pushing a buggy. I say hello, but at the same moment a leaf blower starts up at Appleby Lodge and they don't seem to hear – or see – me. It's possible the sun is in their eyes, although they are both wearing sunglasses.

I unpack my bag and place the books I've brought from the office in a pile on the floor in front of one of the bookcases. I sit down with *The Fourth Protocol* and flick through it. I take out the *Telegraph* crossword. I still don't know or can't remember the capital of Madeira, but maybe if I solve 3 down: Heighten (7), which I think has to be ENHANCE, that tells me 8 across has an H two letters after the N the book's previous owner provided, with ENNUI, and that's enough to remind me that the capital of Madeira is FUNCHAL.

In the kitchen I stick a ready meal in the microwave and while it's warming up I reach for the architects' renderings. I look closely at the two different views of the rear of the main block, the same view I have from my kitchen window. I'm interested in the windows of the second-floor flat to the left of the new lift shaft in the centre of the main block. I noticed before that the windows of the flats in my block are reflected in the windows of the rear of the main block. I know it's ridiculous, but I'm thinking if I could spot my reflection in one of those windows, it would help me with my story, but I hear the ping of the microwave, and, while I'm transferring my meal on to a plate, the voices upstairs start up, back and forth, and this time they're raised, as if one is in the kitchen and the other in the living room, but I still can't tell what they're saying. To try to escape the voices, I take my dinner to my bedroom. It's not very nice but I've got to eat because if I don't Jo will tell me again that I look like I've lost weight. That's if I even see her again. When I've finished I take my plate to the kitchen and while I'm running the hot tap and waiting for it to warm up I look at the architects' renderings again and I realise that one of the garages that has a car sticking out of it is my garage – or their version of my garage. I don't have a car, but I do have a garage. It's filled with boxes of books, of course, that I've attempted to protect against damp by taping plastic bags around them. I look at 'my' garage. The car sticking out of it is a Kia Sportage, which, if I ever had a car, would never be the car I would have, because I wouldn't want a car whose model name I didn't know how to pronounce.

I leave early in the morning. I don't think I want to see Jo again but I do want to get the last of my books from the office, because I really do dislike not finishing things.

I walk through Platt Fields Park and up Heald Place because I don't think I can stand seeing all those driverless cars up and down Curry Mile with their number plates obscured. I'm thinking that even if I invented her, even if she doesn't really exist, Jo is unlikely to be in this early. Yeah, right. A young man in a baseball cap talking on a mobile phone is standing by the entrance to Whitworth Park. I go la-la-la-la in my head as I walk past him, so I don't have to hear what he's saying.

It was another bad night, but at least no one came up from the flat below to bang on my door, or not that I was aware of.

I glance left at the *Snowman*, but don't deviate from the path. As I rejoin Wilmslow Road, in front of the Whitworth Gallery, or the Whitworth as it appears to be called now, I make way for a young couple pushing a buggy. I want to tell them it's not sunny. I see them again outside the Co-op, and then again outside the Royal Northern College of Music. Everywhere I look there are young men in baseball caps talking on mobile phones.

Jo is not in. I get the rest of my books and look around the office for the last time, then leave. At the Walker building I take the stairs and go straight to the third floor. The door to the Apartment is unlocked. I open it and go in and close the door behind me – and lock it. I'm not kidding myself they wouldn't be able to unlock it from the outside, but since there's a lock, I might as well use it. I dump my backpack in the living area, then pick it up again and take it through into the bedroom. I open it and remove the books and put them on the window ledge alongside the other ones. I zip the backpack up and put it between the wardrobe and the chest of drawers where there's a little gap that's just about the right size for it.

I go back into the main room and sit down on the sofa. I concentrate on my ear, but I can't hear or feel anything that I shouldn't be able to hear or feel. I get up and go to the kitchen area and look out of the window. I see the rear elevation of the main block of flats, the glass lift shaft, the garages, the green E-type Jaguar, the two men with their hands in their pockets, the man in the suit with the shaved head, the woman with the ponytail.

Acknowledgements

'Welcome Back' is one of three stories original to this collection; the other two are 'Simister' and 'The Apartment'. 'Safe' was first published in *Confingo*. 'The Child' was written for *The Decadent Handbook* (Dedalus). 'Full on Night' first appeared in *Ambit* and 'Salt' in *Black Static*; both these stories reappeared, in somewhat altered form, in *First Novel* (Vintage).

'Disorder' was Frankensteined out of the lyrics to Joy Division's first album, *Unknown Pleasures*. It uses those words and no others. No words were repeated (unless repeated in the lyrics) and none was excluded (apart from the song titles, which I did not use). It does not, at any point, quote from the lyrics, despite using all the same words (but not in the same order, to paraphrase Eric Morecambe). It was written for and published in *We Were Strangers: Stories Inspired by Unknown Pleasures* (Confingo Publishing) edited by Richard V. Hirst.

The nine sections of 'The Dark Heart' were written to the same length with the intention, where possible, that they be read in random order. At a conference at Edge Hill University in 2016 organised by the European Network for Short Fiction Research, I read the story in place of a keynote speech, the order of the scenes chosen by members of the audience. When the story was published in *Short Fiction in Theory & Practice*, the scenes appeared in the order in which I had written them, but for the story's appearance in this collection, they have again been randomised, the present order determined by dealing nine playing cards that were part of a near-complete pack I found scattered along the paths of Platt Fields Park in Manchester one day in the summer of 2022. The dealing of the cards took place in Mary & Archie, Burton Road, West Didsbury, in September 2022; I shuffled the partial deck, which was then cut by the publisher. As for how many different ways there are in which the story might be read, my daughter, who is very good at maths, tells me that because there are nine sections, there are 362,880 permutations. I totally believe her, but can't get my head around it.

'Insufficient Data for an Image' came about through a collaboration with artist Sian Bonnell. We had paired off as part of a project, Made in Translation, between the Faculty of Arts & Humanities at Manchester Metropolitan University and Manchester's Portico Library, which resulted in an exhibition that ran at the Portico from April to June 2017 curated by Alice Kettle and James Moss. Bonnell and I created a limited-edition book comprising my text and her photographs and video frame grabs.

'Someone Take These Dreams Away' first appeared, as by Marc Werner, in *'68: New Stories From Children of the Revolution* (Salt). 'Maths Tower' was published in *The Flash* (Social Disease) edited by Peter Wild. 'Nothing Else Matters' was a commission for the Chorlton Arts Festival 2015; David Gaffney and Sarah-Clare Conlon invited me to write a new story set in a Chorlton building of my choice. I chose a Wetherspoon's pub, the Sedge Lynn, which I had known in the 80s as the Chorlton Snooker Centre. The story was later published in *Being Dad: Short Stories About Fatherhood* (Tangent) edited by Dan Coxon.

'Strange Times' was a lockdown story, written – or assembled – in lockdown in Manchester, that found a home in *Anglo Files*, a Danish magazine for teachers of English in Denmark. 'Zulu Pond', originally 'Alsiso', was written for *The Alsiso Project*, an anthology edited by Andrew Hook and published by his Elastic Press, in which all the stories had to have the same title: 'Alsiso'. They didn't say you couldn't change the title of your story later. 'The Lancashire Fusilier' was another commissioned story and once again I have to thank David Gaffney, the brains and driving force behind an extraordinary site-specific project at Manchester's Piccadilly Station, which was a Manchester Literature Festival/Bury Text Festival co-production in May 2011. Six writers were invited to pick a location on the station and set and read/perform a story there to an audience watching and listening via wireless headsets. In the 70s I would pay – the price of a platform ticket – to spend hours on Piccadilly Station's platform 5 waiting for – and maybe ultimately cabbing – the Harwich Boat Train. Now someone was paying me to sit there instead. O lucky man!

I am grateful to all the editors, publishers and commissioners named above and below.

Thanks to Tim Shearer of Confingo Publishing, to Confingo art director Zoë McLean, to Confingo force-of-nature Janet Penny; to my former colleagues at the Manchester Writing School; to my agent, John Saddler; to Alison Campbell, John Cavanagh, Ailsa Cox, Andy Cox, Gareth Evans, Adèle Fielding, Michael Hulse, Nigel Kendall, Peter McConville, Tony Lezard, Livi Michael, Danny Moran, Cécile Neyret, Margit Nordskov Nielsen, John Oakey, Brian Radcliffe, Yuka Sonobe, Joe Stretch, Conrad Williams. Special thanks to my wife Ros, to my mum, to Julie, Joanna and Simon, and to my children, Charlie and Bella.

TYPOGRAPHIC DETAILS

Cover Helvetica Neue, Futura PT
Body Helvetica Neue, Baskerville